"I need to talk to you."

Dylan's words carried a foreboding Shaye only was beginning to understand. Did he want to take Timmy away from her?

Stalling, she asked, "Now?"

"Now."

Swallowing hard, she turned away from him and on wobbly legs went down the stairs.

In the living room, Dylan sat on the couch. She perched on the armchair next to it. To her surprise, even that still seemed too close.

"Have you started adoption proceedings yet?"

Her dreams for Timmy were huge, her mind filled with scenes of the two of them facing the world together until Timmy could do it on his own.

She didn't like where this was headed. "I want to. And I know that's what Julia would have wanted, too."

"It is, Shaye?" he returned quickly. "Or deep down in her heart did she want to leave Timmy to me?

"Did she want *me* to be his father?"

CUSTODY
FOR TWO

KAREN ROSE SMITH

Silhouette

SPECIAL EDITION®

Published by Silhouette Books

America's Publisher of Contemporary Romance

SILHOUETTE BOOKS

ISBN 0-373-24753-2

CUSTODY FOR TWO

Copyright © 2006 by Karen Rose Smith

Visit Silhouette Books at www.eHarlequin.com

Printed in U.S.A.

Books by Karen Rose Smith

KAREN ROSE SMITH

read Zane Grey when she was in grade school and loved his books. She also had a crush on Roy Rogers and especially his palomino, Trigger! Around horses as a child, she found them fascinating and intuitive. This series of books set in Wyoming sprang from childhood wishes and adult dreams. When an acquaintance adopted two of the wild mustangs from the western rangelands and invited Karen to visit them, plotlines weren't far behind. For more background on the books in the series, stop by Karen's Web site at www.karenrosesmith.com or write to her at P.O. Box 1545, Hanover, PA 17331.

To Liz Conway—
Thanks for being my lifelong friend.

With thanks to Char Rice who welcomed us
to Cody and enriched our stay there.

With appreciation to Ken Martin who knows
and understands the mustangs so well.
I'll never forget Grey Face and his band.

For information about wild mustangs,
visit www.wildhorsepreservation.com.
For adoption information, go to
www.wildhorseandburro.blm.gov.

Chapter One

He couldn't believe his sister had entrusted her son to Shaye Bartholomew rather than to him. Still in shock even after two days of traveling, Dylan Malloy stepped inside the Neonatal Intensive Care Unit. His gaze focused intently on the woman seated by Timmy's tiny bed…the woman who had custody of his nephew.

Walter Ludlow's call had been a severe blow, and Dylan was still reeling from it. His lawyer and long-time mentor, calling Tasmania from Wild Horse Junction, Wyoming, had hastily told him, "There's no easy way to say this. Julia and Will were in a serious accident. Will died on impact. Julia hung on until Timmy was delivered, then we lost her, too."

We lost her, too.

The words wouldn't fade out. They'd been a shout in Dylan's head ever since he'd heard them. Seconds later Walter had followed them with, "Julia gave Shaye Bartholomew legal guardianship. She didn't want to burden you again."

Dylan couldn't wrap his mind, let alone his heart, around losing Julia. The grief enveloped him like a dark shadow that continuously seeped through him, leaving no room for anything else.

"Fight, Timmy. Fight." Dylan heard Shaye Bartholomew encouraging Timmy, her voice breaking.

The doctor had explained Timmy's condition to Dylan. Born twenty-eight weeks into Julia's pregnancy, he was on a ventilator to help him breathe normally. He had a good chance to survive. But with so many tubes and wires connected to him, that was hard for Dylan to believe.

Did Shaye already think Timmy was hers? he wondered.

She hovered beside the baby, her lips moving silently. Maybe in prayer?

Dylan's work as a wildlife photographer had taught him stillness and patience. But now he had questions, and Shaye Bartholomew held the answers.

After crossing the room, he pulled her attention from the infant bed. "Miss Bartholomew?"

She gave a small sound of surprise when she saw him and recognition dawned. They'd met at Julia's college graduation. Shaye had been a year ahead of his sister, and the two women had become friends.

"Mr. Malloy. I'm so sorry about Julia." Her eyes brimmed with tears.

Why did he suddenly feel as if he wanted to take this woman into his arms to give both of them some comfort?

Dylan knew he looked unkempt. He hadn't shaved in two days, his hair was disheveled and needed a cut, his sweatshirt was streaked with lines from being slept in.

"I got here as soon as I could." He'd been photographing kangaroos when he'd gotten the call. That seemed like eons ago.

Standing, Shaye let him come in closer to Timmy's bed. Dylan could see the reflection of the fluorescent light on her shoulder-length, coffee-brown hair and noticed the sheen in her amber eyes. When their gazes locked, the grief inside him shifted a bit, but he let it settle back into place as he broke eye contact and stared down at his nephew.

Timmy had sandy-brown hair and green eyes…like Julia…like himself.

Softly, Shaye said, "During Julia's pregnancy we talked about baby names. She said she wanted to name a girl after her mother, a boy after her father. *Your* mother and father."

Ironically, like Julia and her husband, their parents had also been killed on a slippery road. That night, Family Services had taken the two of them to a holding facility in Cody. Back then, Dylan had had to break out of his shock to take care of his sister. Now he had to break through it to think about Julia's baby.

Forcing his attention back to Shaye, Dylan couldn't keep the edge from his tone when he said, "I want to know how you came to be named Timmy's guardian. I know Will's mother was too frail to consider—"

One of the monitors began to beep loudly. At once, a nurse appeared at Timmy's bedside while another rushed to call a doctor.

A physician in a white coat hurried in. One of the nurses put a hand on Shaye's arm and spoke to Dylan. "Please wait outside."

"I want to know what's happening," Dylan demanded, fear for his nephew beating hard against his chest.

"We have to let them work." Shaye tugged at Dylan's elbow. "They know what they're doing. The doctor will come talk to us when they get him stabilized. We have to do what's best for him. We're just in the way."

After another glance at the personnel around the baby's bed, certainty dawned that he *was* in the way. Dylan pulled from Shaye's clasp and strode to the door leading outside the unit.

Had Dylan Malloy come back to mourn his sister? Or had he returned to Wild Horse Junction to claim his nephew?

Shaye took a few shallow breaths, reaching deep inside for the strength that had kept her going since the call about Julia and Will. Once in the hall, she motioned to the waiting room.

Instead of going in, Dylan paced. "I don't want to be that far away." His gaze shot back to the NICU. "Surely someone will tell us if he's going to make it."

When he ran his hand through his tawny hair, when she glimpsed again the primordial pain in his green eyes, she wished she could ease his grief. But no one could. "Have you spoken with the doctor?"

"When I was waiting for my flight in London."

"Then you know this is all up to Timmy—how he responds to the antibiotics and the help they're giving him."

"I understand that. I certainly *don't* understand everything else. Why did Will have Julia out in bad weather? She was almost seven months pregnant, for God's sake!"

Understandably, Dylan was looking for somebody to blame, as people did when tragedy struck, and goodness knew Dylan and Julia had already experienced plenty of it. All Shaye could do was to tell him what she knew.

"Julia had been cooped up inside for over a week due to the bad weather. Will wouldn't even let her step onto a snowy sidewalk because he was afraid she'd fall. But she was going stir crazy. The morning of—" Shaye's voice broke in spite of her effort to put her own emotion aside.

Clearing her throat, she went on. "The morning of the accident, I stopped in to see her. She was in such a good mood. She said she'd cajoled Will into taking her to the Johnsons that night. The weather was supposed to hold and not turn until early morning."

"The Johnsons practically live in the mountains," Dylan muttered. "Those roads can be treacherous any time of the year, let alone when there's snow on them." He swore and turned away from her.

Unexpectedly, Shaye didn't know what to do, and that was unusual for her. In her job as a social worker, she routinely handled sticky situations. But this one was personal. Something about this man touched her in an elemental way, and that, as well as the crisis with Timmy, made her uncertain.

Dylan faced her again, everything about him shouting restrained energy, restrained emotion, restrained frustration. "Did you know Julia was going to name you as guardian?"

"Yes, I did," she answered quietly, bracing herself for whatever came next.

The nerve in his jaw worked. "Julia spoke often of you, Miss Bartholomew. I know you were good friends. But I need to know how this…legacy came about."

"It's Shaye," she murmured, needing to be on a first-name basis without knowing why. With a nod, she motioned to the lounge again. "Let's sit down."

After a glance at the NICU, he followed her into the waiting room. Although she lowered herself onto one of the fabric-covered chairs, Dylan remained standing. She felt like a schoolgirl sitting in front of a principal, which was ridiculous. In her position as caseworker for the department of family services in the county, she'd learned to stand her ground. With two brothers to take care of, she'd had to be assertive or she would have been snowed under or trampled. However, in the presence of Dylan Malloy, her confidence seemed to vanish.

Taking a breath, she plunged in. "You know Julia and I met in college."

He nodded, waiting.

"Since we were both from Wild Horse Junction, we caught rides together from Laramie to come home. At first I thought she was reserved. Then I found out she just used reserve to protect herself. She told me about what happened to your parents and about spending time in foster care."

She remembered the story Julia had related about how Dylan and Walter Ludlow had become friends. At eighteen, Dylan had just graduated from high school and landed a job at the local paper. He'd walked into the attorney's office saying, "I need a lawyer to petition the court to become my sister's legal guardian."

Julia had been eight and Dylan sixteen when they'd been orphaned, and Dylan had known his sister was unbearably unhappy in foster care. He'd moved heaven and earth to gain custody of her. He'd made sure she was safe, happy and secure until she'd gone to college. Then he'd left Wild Horse Junction to follow his own dreams.

"Julia never stopped telling me how grateful she was that you rescued her," she added softly.

"Not soon enough," he murmured, as if he was remembering all too well.

"As soon as you could."

Seeming to ignore her comment, he said evenly, "After you graduated, you went on for your masters."

"That's right. By the time I returned to Wild Horse, Julia had met Will and they'd eloped."

"She told me she didn't want a big fancy wedding," Dylan mused. "I wanted to give her one."

"I think Julia and Will just wanted to start their life without fanfare. So many times she told me she wanted a home and family and someplace to belong."

"She knew she could count on me," Dylan insisted.

"Yes, she knew that, but she also realized you'd sacrificed for her for eight years. Eight years you put your dreams aside for her. She knew how much being a wildlife photographer meant to you."

"Not as much as she did," he protested quickly.

"You proved that," Shaye reassured him. "You stayed here and worked on the paper when all you wanted to do was to catch a plane to someplace exotic."

His green eyes became piercing in their intensity. "You seem to know a lot about me." He rubbed the back of his neck. "It's an uncomfortable feeling when I don't know *you*. Have you had experience taking care of kids?"

"In my job I sometimes have to. But besides that— My mother died when I was ten. I had brothers who were eight and five. My father, a cardiologist, was gone a lot, so I had to take care of them."

"On your own?"

"No, he hired a housekeeper, but she didn't tell bedtime stories or know where they left their favorite toy. She didn't take the time to make peanut butter and marshmallow crackers or help them build a clubhouse."

"You were a sister and a mother hen?" Dylan asked perceptively.

"Sometimes that boundary blurred. I'm not so sure my brothers didn't resent it as much as appreciate it."

Dylan looked across the room out the window, as if trying to see into the past—perhaps the years in foster care…the years when Julia was his life…the years when he pursued his vocation. "I never tried to be a father to Julia. We were brother and sister and that was the only bond we needed. At least, I thought so."

Now she could see he was thinking about Timmy and maybe wondering exactly why Julia had asked her to be guardian rather than him. She had explained, but maybe that explanation hadn't been enough.

Footsteps sounded outside the waiting room and Dr. Carrera stepped inside. "We've got Timmy stabilized again and we're monitoring him closely. I think it would be better for you *and* him if you just give us some time here. Take a break. Get something to eat or take a walk."

"What if something happens?" She'd been staying close, hoping in some way would help.

"I have your cell phone number," the physician said kindly.

"You have mine, too," Dylan interjected gruffly. "I left it with the nurses at the desk."

The doctor looked from one of them to the other. "Legally, I know Shaye is the guardian, but I realize, Mr. Malloy, you are the blood relative. Is there something I should know about?"

When Dylan moved, he did so agilely, like one of the beautiful animals he photographed. A male tiger came to Shaye's mind.

Standing beside the doctor now, Dylan shoved his hands into the pockets of his cargo pants. "I found out about Julia on Sunday. I didn't even have time to shower or change before I left Tasmania, and I didn't sleep on the plane. I haven't had a chance to absorb the fact that I don't have a sister anymore, let alone the surprise that she wanted Shaye to be the baby's parent. Shaye and I need time to talk."

He glanced at her over his shoulder. "How about a walk outside?"

Most men would probably have asked her to share a cup of coffee either in the hospital cafeteria or in the family restaurant across the street. But not Dylan Malloy.

He wanted to take a walk on a cold February evening in Wyoming. Her royal blue parka hung on an old-fashioned brass coatrack in the corner. A leather bomber jacket hung there, too, and she assumed it was Dylan's.

Dylan's gaze passed over her cranberry blouse and her navy slacks as well as her black shoelike boots.

"Do you *mind* going for a walk?" he asked her. "I suppose we could stay here and talk."

She'd seen nothing but the confines of the hospital for the past two days. Even last night she'd curled up on the couch to get some sleep. She needed the cold to clear her head as much as he did.

Standing, she went to the rack for her parka. "I could use some fresh air."

"If anything else occurs, I have your numbers," the neonatologist said diplomatically, and disappeared down the hall.

Neither of them spoke as they walked to the elevator. Dylan pressed the button. Shaye wrapped her scarf around her neck then pulled her hair from under it. Reaching into her pocket, she found her knit hat and pulled it onto her head.

When they stepped into the elevator, she could feel Dylan's gaze on her and she realized her whole body was responding to it...to him. She was warmer than she should have been and she attributed that to nerves, anxiety about Timmy and everything else that had happened. Certainly a man couldn't make her warmer just by *looking* at her. That had never happened with Chad, although she'd considered herself in love with him. She'd thought he was madly in love with her. She'd been wrong. Yes, she'd loved *him,* but apparently Chad had seen her as convenient and disposable.

Why was she thinking about that now when there were so many other things to think about...so many things to feel? Whenever she stopped thinking, she started feeling. Missing Julia, realizing Timmy would never know his real mother, made her sick inside.

Aware of the bulk of Dylan beside her, she felt awkwardly self-conscious. She usually knew what to say and how to say it. Why not now? Because the stakes were so high and involved her becoming a mother? Because the grief they shared could form a bond neither of them might want?

In the lobby, she pulled on tan leather gloves.

"Are you sure you want to do this?" he asked. "Hiking is a habit for me. It's the way I catch the right photograph, the way I solve a problem or find an answer."

She couldn't keep her gaze from passing over the thick hair that fell across his forehead and shagged over his collar. His hands were bare though he did wear rugged-looking shoes. "Aren't you going to be cold? It will soon be dark and there's a wind."

"I don't think a stroll around the hospital will do me in."

According to his sister, this man had climbed a glacier to get a particular shot. Her worry for him was unwarranted. "I didn't mean to suggest—"

He held up a hand to stay her words...as an apology for his sharpness.

Looking into his very green eyes, she saw his anguish over Julia as well as Timmy. "It's okay. Come on."

They headed for the door.

Nestled at the foot of the Painted Peak Mountains, Wild Horse Junction had been born in the eighteen hundreds and some of the original buildings had survived. The town was a mixture of old-fashioned and modern, classic and contemporary—from Clementine's, the saloon turned honky-tonk and now modern day bar and grill, to a saddle shop, trading post, discount store and modern hospital. Wild Horse had a little bit of everything.

Thank goodness Wild Horse Junction's St. Luke's Hospital had a Neonatal Intensive Care Unit. The unit was only three years old. A few years ago, a celebrity who spent summers on her ranch in Cody had been passing through Wild Horse Junction when she'd gone into premature labor. There had been complications, but the obstetrician at St. Luke's had saved both the actress and her baby. To show her gratitude she had endowed the hospital with a Neonatal Intensive Care Unit. Although Wild Horse Junction was still basically a small town, it had become a center in Wyoming for babies born at risk.

Shaye'd thought about leaving Wild Horse once. She would have had to, to follow Chad. But she hadn't really wanted to. Her family was here. Her good friends, Gwen and Kylie, whom she'd known since grade school, were still here. During tourist season, all kinds of people came and went, and she found them interesting and exciting. Yet most of them left and *she* stayed. That was the way she liked it.

Unlike Dylan Malloy.

Julia had told her how he'd dreamed of getting away from the time he was a small child, from the time his father had bought him his first camera.

"A walk around the hospital or across the street to the park?" Dylan asked as they exited the building.

"To the park."

Wild Horse Junction's park was an unusual one. The town had been named for the wild mustangs that used to roam the Painted Peaks but now mostly lived in the Big Horn Mountains about an hour away. Bronze sculptures of the beautiful animals had been added to the park since the early nineteen hundreds. Black wrought-iron benches were plentiful and every spring the city council made sure they were refurbished and kept in good shape for the residents come summer.

She could imagine bringing Timmy here, walking him in a stroller. When he grew older, she could see him playing on the swings at the south end of the park. During the past two days she'd purposely created pictures in her head of the future, believing they'd come true. The pictures eased her loss and kept her away from the truth that she'd never see Julia or Will Grayson again. Her eyes burned from the tears she'd shed and she almost wished she could go numb instead of having to deal with the depths of loss.

Traffic was sporadic as she and Dylan stood at an intersection to cross the street. They'd just stepped off the curb when an SUV suddenly rounded the corner and sped by them. Dylan reached for Shaye's elbow, holding it protectively to let her know when it was safe to cross. Unlikely as the sensation was, she seemed to feel the heat from his long fingers and his large hand through the down of her jacket.

As if he sensed something, too, he looked at her, and even though the night was turning dark and shadowy, she caught an awareness on his face...some kind of current between them.

Flustered, she hurried with him across the street, his long strides making her quicken hers. As they entered the park's winding stone-covered path, snow began to fall lightly. Shaye lifted her face and the feel of the flakes somehow seemed to cleanse her of the chaos of the past few days.

As Dylan stopped, he said huskily, "I wish I had my camera."

"Why?"

"Because I never took a shot of a woman looking exactly like that—like you were with your face tipped up to the sky."

Frissons of excitement shot through Shaye and she didn't know how to respond. "Do you photograph people much? The shots in magazines Julia showed me were mostly of animals."

"Most people like to have their picture taken. I'd rather have the challenge of capturing an animal unaware of me, photographing it in its real home, snapping interaction with the other animals. It's all genuine and honest."

"Unlike people?"

"People are much more complicated. Much of what they do is motivated by something."

"Like?" she coaxed.

"Do you deal with foster families much?"

"I do."

"Talk about motives. I know the system is over-crowded. I know there's constantly a need for placing kids. But neither Julia nor I had pleasant experiences. The families we were placed in weren't motivated by compassion."

"Julia told me the foster father in the family she was placed in drank. And when he did, he became loud and abusive."

"That's right," Dylan confirmed. "I had to get her out of there."

"What about the family *you* were placed with?"

He shook his head as if his experience hadn't mattered. "I wasn't there that long."

"Two years can feel like forever when you're not happy."

Stopping again, he said, "You're perceptive."

"I have to be, in my work. I have to use my intuition as much as my training."

When he stared down at her, he admitted, "The family I was with just wanted the money they received every month. I was good for chores and work around the house, but there was no real caring there."

"I'm sorry," Shaye said, meaning it.

"That's long ago and I've forgotten about it. But I saw firsthand that altruism isn't part of what most people are about."

"You weren't thinking about yourself when you made a life for you and Julia."

"She was my sister."

Shaye could tell that was the only explanation he intended to give.

They walked for a few minutes under Russian olive trees catching the snow. Aspen branches waved in the breeze.

"Do you think she had a premonition?" Dylan asked suddenly. "Do you think that's why she chose a guardian before the baby was born?"

"I don't know. I do know Julia wouldn't take any chances with a child, that she would have secured the baby's future no matter what she had to do."

Stopping again, he took Shaye by the arm and looked deeply into her eyes. "You're a single woman. You have a career. Do you *want* to be a mother to Timmy?"

This was the moment where she had to make everything she said matter. Aware of Dylan's hand on her arm and the magnetic pull of his gaze, her curiosity about him was growing. She tamped it down.

"I want to be Timmy's mother with all my heart and soul. I'll do everything in my power to make sure he grows up to be a man Julia would be proud of."

Dylan's jaw set as he studied her and analyzed her words. The white of his breath seemed to mingle with the puff of hers as a bond formed. It was a bond that she knew she didn't want…yet couldn't break.

With a slight nod, he broke eye contact and dropped his hand to his side. "Let's go back."

She knew there was *no* going back. And that truth scared her as much as her visceral reaction to Dylan Malloy.

* * *

"You need to go to your apartment and get some sleep," Walter Ludlow warned Dylan later that night.

Dylan paced the lawyer's home office. His friend was a widower now and lived in one of the brick row homes not far from the center of town.

"I'm going back to the hospital," he said resolutely.

"You're not going to do that baby any good if you run yourself into the ground."

Dylan hadn't even been back to his apartment yet, hadn't been there for six months. His luggage, laptop and camera gear were still in the trunk of the rental car he'd secured at the airport so he could drive to the hospital in a hurry.

After his walk with Shaye, he'd spent an hour with her sitting by Timmy's bed. She'd finally left to get something to eat and when she'd returned, he'd come to Walter's.

"I'm used to sleeping on sofas or cots or on the ground. Camping out in a chair in a waiting room isn't going to kill me. Timmy's in crisis right now and every hour matters. I have to do this for Julia."

"You have to take care of yourself for Julia. She'd want that."

Dylan's adrenaline was pumping full-speed. He stopped pacing and made himself sit on the edge of a leather chair in front of Walter's desk. "I thought I knew my sister inside and out, but this will of hers— Maybe I should find a PI and have him run a report on Shaye Bartholomew."

"Don't waste your money," Walter advised him. "I've

known Shaye's family all my life. Carson Bartholomew has never been the best father. He's a cardiac surgeon, so you can imagine the hours he keeps. He never saw much of his kids *before* his wife died, let alone after."

"How did Shaye's mother die?"

"A brain aneurysm she never knew she had. She just fell asleep one night and didn't wake up again. After that, Carson saw to the kids' physical needs but not much else. Although he hired a housekeeper, Shaye did the mothering, the cooking, the shopping and anything else that needed to be done. That's what made her become a social worker, and a damn good one. I've been involved in some of the cases she's handled. So don't think a PI's report is going to give you any more than I can tell you. She's a good woman, Dylan. She was a good friend to Julia, and I think your sister knew what she was doing."

Dylan's head jerked up as his eyes met Walter's. "You don't think I deserve custody?"

"This isn't a matter of deserving, boy. Julia loved you. She wanted the best life for you. She knows your blood's in your work. Why would she want to saddle you with a baby? On the other hand, if Timmy's with Shaye, you can be involved in his life as much as you want to be when you're here. I'm sure she wouldn't turn you away. That's not Shaye, and Julia knew it."

"I feel as if I have a responsibility—"

Walter cut him off. "You fulfilled your responsibility when you took Julia in and cared for her. Don't be a martyr."

Walter had never pulled punches with him and now, for the first time all day, Dylan relaxed into the chair, realizing how tired he was. Looking down at his clothes, he imagined the sight he made, needing a shave and a haircut. More than that, he needed a shower and a couple of hours of sound sleep. Maybe he could catch a few winks at the hospital.

He wasn't a martyr, but he *did* care.

Standing, he zippered his jacket. "I'm going to run by my apartment to make sure everything's still in one piece and take a shower. But if you want me, I'll be at the hospital."

"You always were stubborn," Walter muttered.

"I've had to be." Crossing to the door of Walter's den, Dylan said, "Thanks for everything you've done. I'll keep you informed."

When Dylan left his friend's house, wind buffeted him as pictures of Julia played in his mind—how happy she'd been when she'd come to live with him, how she'd cooked for him, how she'd chewed the end of her pencil as she'd solved math problems. He hadn't come home this Christmas. He'd planned his schedule to take a break when his nephew was born.

Dylan's eyes burned. He was just too damned tired.

As he climbed into the rental vehicle, in spite of his worry over Timmy, he saw Shaye's face as she'd lifted it to the snowflakes. Switching on the ignition, he blanked out the image, needing to keep on an even keel, needing to forget that when he'd touched Shaye Bartholomew, everything inside him had gone on alert.

She's just another woman.

But then he thought about his sister's fondness for Shaye and her decision to leave her child to her friend. In turmoil, in spite of Walter Ludlow's words, Dylan knew the next few days would be crucial in making his decision on whether to stay in Wild Horse Junction or go back to the life he'd come to love.

Chapter Two

As Dylan carried the last of his gear into his apartment, the space definitely had the feel of a bachelor pad not lived in for six months. Situated on the second floor of a rambling old farmhouse on the outskirts of town, Dylan kept it for when he returned to the area. The retired farmer who lived on the first floor kept watch for him and sent someone in to clean once a month when he wasn't home. It had always suited his purposes just fine.

Yet now the place held so many memories of Julia and her years with him that he felt bombarded. Although he could now indulge in a bit of luxury if he wanted to, he hadn't. Practically furnished when Julia had lived here, he'd replaced the second-hand sofa with a more contemporary comfortable one. The TV and sound system sitting on pine shelves were utilitarian, too, rather than up to date. Julia had bought the setup for him one Christmas after she and Will were married. His small kitchen with its bar and stools was functional, and he still slept in the thrift-shop bed he'd bought after he'd landed his first job. The second bedroom, which had been his sister's, was now filled with file cabinets that stored transparencies and negatives. Cartons of photographic equipment were stacked in any spare space. A third bedroom was occupied with state-of-the-art equipment—computer, scanner, two printers and a fax machine. Julia had often shaken her head with a smile and told him he should invest in drapes rather than update his computer. But he never had.

In spite of the memories, the unlived-in feel of the apartment bothered him now, when it never had before. Because he'd lost Julia and she'd never be calling to chat with him again while he worked? She'd never be testing out a new recipe on him when he was home? She'd never be—

The thoughts tightened his chest and made breathing difficult.

After Dylan turned up the heat, he stripped off his clothes and showered, letting the sluicing hot water splash away images that were just too painful.

He'd found a pair of clean jeans and was pulling on a tan-colored, long-sleeved flannel shirt when his cell phone beeped. He'd placed it in the charger on the bedroom dresser. He picked it up, bracing himself as he switched it on.

"Mr. Malloy? It's Dr. Carrera."

Dylan's heart hammered faster. "Yes, Doctor."

"What's your blood type?"

"AB positive."

"Good. Timmy is anemic and we think a transfusion will help. Fortunately he's AB positive, too. Would you be willing to give blood? Or should we go to the blood bank?"

"Of course, I'll give blood. I'll be there in five minutes." Something about giving his life force to his nephew seemed right.

"Careful on the roads, Mr. Malloy. Snow's making them slick and we don't want any further tragedies."

Further tragedies. Such a generic way of putting it. The words didn't begin to cover what Dylan was feeling.

"Is Miss Bartholomew still there?" he asked before the doctor hung up.

"Yes, she is. She also wanted to volunteer for a transfusion but she's not a match."

A picture of Shaye was beginning to form in his mind; a picture of a woman who was a caregiver. He hadn't known many women like that in his life and neither had Julia. Maybe that's why his sister had gravitated toward Shaye.

Thinking first and foremost about the transfusion he was going to give Timmy, Dylan grabbed his jacket, wallet and keys and headed for the hospital.

When Dylan met Dr. Carrera in the emergency room, he asked, "Is this really going to help?"

"I'm hoping it will. Nothing in medicine is a certainty."

"Nothing in *life* is a certainty," Dylan muttered.

The staff was pleasant and friendly, but Dylan wished he was anywhere but here.

That was especially so a half hour later when Shaye peeked into the cubicle. "How are you doing?" she asked.

They'd just removed the paraphernalia needed to withdraw his blood. He was glad Shaye hadn't stopped in five minutes sooner when he'd been flat on his back. He didn't like the idea of her seeing him as anything but strong.

"I'm fine. The toughest part of this is signing all the paperwork," he joked. "There's more red tape in giving blood than in applying for a visa."

Coming into the room, she shrugged. "I wouldn't know about that. I've never been out of the U.S."

Rolling down the sleeve of his flannel shirt, he buttoned the cuff. "Did you ever want to see the rest of the world?"

"Not really." She came a few steps closer. "I went to a conference in New York City once and hated it. Too much hustle and bustle. I've also been to California, and that was okay. There's some pretty scenery there, especially around Big Sur. But I love the mountains and the plains and the hot springs, the cactus and sage. I love the old-fashioned flavor of this town and its history." She shrugged again. "I'm happy here."

Her hair brushing against her cheek distracted Dylan. So did the pretty amber of her eyes. "I guess that's the difference between us. I was never happy here. I always wanted more. I wanted to run free, stopping when I pleased, moving on when I liked."

"Like the wild mustangs," she remarked softly.

A nurse bustled in, bringing Dylan a glass of juice. He drank it quickly, handing the glass back with a thank-you.

She'd disappeared when Shaye said, "Julia didn't feel like that at all. She didn't want to wander, either. Maybe it's a woman thing. I've met other men who seem to be searching for something."

The way she said it, wandering was a dirty word. "I don't think needing space and wanting to travel has anything to do with being male or female," he protested, reading an underlying message in what Shaye had said…a possible story in her background.

As he stood, he felt almost exhausted.

She was by his side in an instant. "You're looking kind of gray. Are you okay?"

"Just tired. I'm going to bunk on the sofa upstairs in the waiting room."

Still gazing at him with those beautiful, soft, golden-brown eyes, she asked, "When was the last time you ate?"

Before he could answer, a tall, husky, bearded man in a parka appeared in the doorway. "I could ask *you* the same question."

Shaye turned at the sound of an obviously familiar voice. "Randall! What are you doing here?"

"Barb sent me. She said I should hogtie you if I had to and drag you back to our place for a decent meal. You can't live here twenty-four hours a day. Those are her words *and* mine. What are you doing down here, anyway? One of the nurses pointed me in this direction."

As Shaye studied the older of her two brothers, she realized he looked as if he should work in a logging camp. Instead, he was an X-ray technician and had probably just gotten off duty.

Turning to Dylan, Shaye said, "Dylan, this is my brother, Randall. Randall, this is Julia's brother, Dylan Malloy. He just gave blood for Timmy."

"I see." After he extended his condolences and Dylan thanked him, Randall glanced at Shaye thoughtfully, then back at Dylan. "You *are* looking a bit gray around the gills. Why don't you come along with us? My wife always has a refrigerator full of leftovers."

"I'll grab something in the cafeteria," Dylan answered, looking uncomfortable.

"The cafeteria is closed," Shaye told him. "You'd have to get one of those dry sandwiches out of the vending machines. Come with us. We don't have to be gone long. You'll feel better once you've eaten."

As soon as Shaye said the words, she knew they weren't true. Nothing could help the way Dylan was feeling. But the food *would* help keep his body strong…and hers, too.

Dylan mulled over her advice. "I want to go upstairs first and talk to Dr. Carrera."

"We can do that. Randall, if you don't want to wait, I can drive us over."

"I want to know how Timmy's doing, too. I can wait, then I can drive you back."

Unsettled by her reaction to Julia's brother, Shaye watched him carefully as they all got into the elevator and went upstairs, grateful Randall was along. With a chaperone of sorts, she didn't have to worry so much about the increase of her pulse or the excitement that tingled through her when she was close to Dylan. However, when Randall gave her an interested glance, she knew that might not be true. In the close quarters of the elevator, she could feel a pull toward Dylan that shocked her. If she had to admit it, she'd felt that same pull at Julia's graduation when she'd met him, and had run from it.

She'd known what Dylan Malloy did for a living and she'd wanted no part of an involvement with a man like him.

A half hour later Dylan found himself seated at Barb and Randall Bartholomew's kitchen table, enjoying a dinner of warmed-up barbecued back ribs, parsley potatoes and green beans. Shaye was daintily cutting meat off her ribs with a knife and fork while he just picked up a portion. Maybe he'd become less civilized in his travels, not in tune with the needs of humans but rather in tune with the animals he photographed.

"We're ready for bed, Mommy," came a childish girl's voice from the upstairs of the old Victorian house. Dylan had met Barb and Randall's kids briefly when he'd come in. They were six and seven, and as soon as they'd found out he photographed animals, they'd been full of questions until Randall had shooed them off to get ready for bed.

"I'll be up in a minute," Barb called.

"I'll go with you." Randall pointed to the chocolate-chip brownies sitting on a dish on the counter. "Help yourselves," he said with a wink as he and Barb left the kitchen and went to put their kids to bed.

Left alone with Shaye, uncomfortable silence fell between them. "They're nice people," Dylan commented.

"My brother used to be a real bug when we were growing up. He pushed the limits as far as he could to see if I could handle him or if I had to bring Dad in on it. But he's mellowing with age."

"Or maybe *you* are," Dylan responded, recognizing changes in himself…in his way of thinking as he'd gotten older.

She gave a little laugh. "I guess that's true."

After Dylan finished his potatoes, he kept the conversation rolling, not only to fill the silence but because he wanted to know more about Shaye. "Randall mentioned he's an X-ray technician."

She set her fork beside her plate. "Yes, he is. He didn't want to be a rancher or to run a small business. He liked the medical field but he certainly didn't want the hours our father put in. He and Barb met in high school, so he didn't want to spend too many years studying, either. Becoming an X-ray technician seemed to be a good compromise."

"Does Barb work?"

"No, she's always been available for the kids, helping out at the school. But…"

"But?"

"She's volunteered to take care of Timmy for me once he's out of the hospital…once I go back to work."

"You're making plans." Dylan's voice was low as he realized how Shaye's life was going to change.

"I have to. I have to believe everything will work out.

I don't know how long Timmy will be in the hospital. After he comes home I'll take a couple of months off and then go back about thirty hours a week for a while."

Suddenly he thought about Timmy's inheritance and what that could mean to Shaye. "Timmy will inherit everything of Julia's and Will's." He watched her carefully to gauge her reaction.

"Yes, he will. But all of that will go into an account for his education. I don't want to touch it."

After Dylan thought that over, he asked, "Has Will's mother been to the hospital to see Timmy? I know her arthritis limits her mobility."

"She was in this morning, but it's so painful for her to look at him. She remembers everything she's lost. She'll be returning to Nebraska right after the service. I promised her I'd call her often to let her know how Timmy is doing."

Dylan knew he had to bring up what he'd been thinking and feeling. "I don't know if it's right for me to let you do this. I'm Timmy's uncle and he should be *my* responsibility."

Shaye's face went pale. "A child has to be more than a responsibility, and I think Julia knew that. She also knew I love children and I'd cherish one of my own—not just feel responsible. Eventually, I'm going to file for adoption, but not until Timmy's healthy and everything's on an even keel. I *want* to be Timmy's mother."

Something else had been bothering Dylan. "Are you involved with anyone?" He didn't care if the question sounded blunt because he needed to know. A beautiful woman like Shaye certainly didn't sit alone on her free nights.

"No, I'm not," she answered easily. "I can give all my time and attention to Timmy. You don't have to worry about that."

"I wasn't worried. I was more concerned your significant other wouldn't be able to accept a child not his flesh and blood." He couldn't bear to leave Timmy in a situation like that.

"I'm not involved with anyone," she said again.

"Surely, you date."

"Actually, I don't very much. My work takes up a lot of my time…at least, it did before Timmy. And I socialize with my good friends on weekends, or with my family. I have a full life, Dylan. I don't need a man in it."

"You don't *need* a man in it, or you don't *want* a man in it?" Now his interest was piqued. Was Shaye just a typical modern woman who could find happiness on her own? Or was there a reason behind her independence?

She pushed her plate back and crossed her arms in front of her on the table. "You're fishing. What do you want to know?"

In spite of himself, Dylan had to smile. He liked Shaye's up-front attitude. "I'm wondering if you had a bad experience that made you create your life the way it is."

When she tucked her silky hair behind one ear, the wave of it curled on her shoulder. "I was involved with someone when I was in college. It didn't end well."

If he wasn't careful, he knew she'd clam up and not tell him more. "When you were an undergrad?" he asked.

"No, when I was working on my master's degree. He was a guest lecturer—an archeologist."

Sensing Shaye wouldn't go on unless he poked a bit,

he did. "He wanted you to leave Wild Horse Junction with him, but you wanted to stay here."

"Not exactly. I loved him. I thought we were building something important. I would have gone with him if he had asked. But he didn't ask. He received a grant for a dig in India, and he didn't even consider taking me with him."

"Maybe he guessed you wouldn't be happy."

"I never had a chance to find out...because apparently his feelings for me weren't as deep as mine were for him."

Although Shaye had recounted her story as if it were old history, Dylan could hear the refrain of betrayal that ran through it—the pain that had never completely gone away.

"How about you?" she asked.

He'd left himself wide open for that one. "My life hasn't been conducive to serious involvement."

"But it is to *non*-serious involvement?"

The hint of disapproval in the question had him watching how he answered. "Even a wanderer needs company besides his camera now and then." Though truth be told, that kind of company wore thin and he'd rather be alone or trekking after a photograph he'd never taken before.

As if his answer disturbed her, Shaye restlessly re-arranged her silverware, stood and picked up the plate of brownies on the counter. When she brought them over to the table, she set them in front of him.

"Not interested?" he asked with a half-smile.

"I don't give in to chocolate cravings often because I know it's habit-forming."

"I admire your willpower."

"I'm not sure willpower has anything to do with it." She smiled back. "I'm just vain."

"I doubt that."

She looked up at him, surprised. "Why would you say that?"

"Because selfish people are vain, and I already know that you're not selfish."

Her cheeks took on some color. Leaning away from him and their conversation, she began to clear the table. "We'd better get back to Timmy. I don't want to be gone too long."

"Neither do I." Timmy was the only essence of Julia he had left. Seeing him made losing Julia even more real. But seeing him also reminded Dylan the baby was an essential part of his sister that he could hold on to.

Dylan's deep, heartfelt words turned Shaye to face him once again. Their gazes locked and held. A vision of holding Shaye in his sleeping bag under the stars was so incredibly real, he ached to do it. His physical response was so strong that he set his brownie back on the plate. It seemed the pain he was experiencing over the loss of his sister was rebounding into an attraction to Shaye.

Breaking eye contact, he muttered, "I think I'll skip dessert, too." She obviously knew what was good for *her.* Dylan reminded himself what was good for *him.* While he was in Wild Horse Junction, Timmy was his main concern…his *only* concern.

Dylan stood in the NICU, looking down at his nephew. He'd let Shaye visit first since he needed a little time to prepare. He wasn't sure what he'd prepared for because the sight of the tiny baby on the ventilator to help him breathe was heartbreaking. All Dylan could do was wish Timmy life, wish him good health, wish Timmy could have known his mother and father. Dylan had long ago stopped praying, stopped believing that someone had a master plan.

After losing his parents, after losing Julia to the foster care system for a while, he'd known a man created his own destiny. If he didn't take control of it, others would. Now, standing beside Timmy's bed, he wished he could believe that prayer could make a difference. He wished he could believe that one day he'd see his parents and Julia again.

After his visiting time with Timmy was up, he went to the waiting room. Shaye wasn't there, though her coat hung beside his on the rack. By the time he crossed to the window to look down on the lamplit street, Shaye came through the door, her arms full of pillows and blankets.

"I thought we might need these."

He'd been in such shock when he'd first arrived, confused by his sister's decision, that he hadn't completely appreciated Shaye's beauty. In spite of that, her presence had impacted him and now he realized why. Her silky burnished-brown hair moved around her face when she walked. He'd seen amber mined from the earth that was the rich color of her golden-brown eyes. When he was close enough to her, he could just make out the smattering of almost invisible freckles on her cheeks. From what he could tell, she didn't use makeup to try to cover anything, and he liked that natural look.

Now, as she walked across the room, he couldn't help but admire her trim figure.

He glanced again at her arms full of blankets and pillows. There was one long sofa in the waiting room and several chairs.

"I'll push two of the chairs together," Dylan told her as he slipped a pillow and blanket from her arms.

"You won't be able to sleep like that."

"I've slept on worse. Don't forget, I'm used to a tent."

"Whether you want to admit it or not," Shaye argued with him, "you're practically dead on your feet. I'm not there yet, but getting there fast."

She glanced at the sofa. "I checked to see if they had any of those recliners we could wheel in, but they're all in use. We'll have to share. From the looks of the sofa, we can both stretch out." When she added the last with a little smile, he realized he liked her positive outlook. He liked a lot of things about her.

"We can try it," he said doubtfully. "On the other hand, you could go back to your place and get a good night's sleep. I'll call you if anything happens."

"Or you could go back to your place and *I* could call *you*."

Already Dylan knew Shaye wouldn't budge on this. "The sofa it is," he decided, going to it and shaking out the blanket.

The whole idea of sharing the sofa seemed like a common sense one until Shaye plunked on one end and looked at him as if to figure out how to accomplish the feat.

"You can put your legs on the inside," he suggested. Propping her pillow against the arm of the sofa, she swung her legs up close to the back. "It's a good thing this is wide."

"And long," Dylan remarked, lying back against his pillow.

After he swung his feet up beside Shaye's hip, he crossed one over the other to take up less room. She was small and he was long. Somehow they seemed to fit like two puzzle pieces. The thing was, his legs were smack against hers. Even with corduroy and denim between them, he found he couldn't help but imagine the curve of her leg, the probable smoothness of her skin.

Aroused, he picked up the blanket and tossed it over them. He'd simply been without a woman for too long. That was all. However, as he lay there, he could smell the traces of a sweet, rose-scented perfume that did as much to arouse him as her leg against his. He'd noticed it earlier and wondered if it was shampoo or lotion or perfume. Wondering about it brought other visions he didn't want to entertain—Shaye smoothing lotion on her arms, Shaye dabbing perfume on her pulse points, Shaye under the shower washing her hair…

Damn! He must be more than sleep deprived if he couldn't control the path of his thoughts. Dylan considered himself flexible, but he always liked to be in control. Since he'd returned to Wild Horse Junction, he didn't seem to have any control. He'd left the small town to run his own life…to find freedom…to take what he wanted in a world that was so big he couldn't explore it all.

Uncomfortable silence filled the waiting room. Dylan didn't move, not wanting to remind himself of how close Shaye was. His mind told him to close his eyes so his body could sleep.

Instead of closing his eyes, curiosity nudged him to ask, "You said you have another brother besides Randall?"

"Yes, I do."

"What does the other one do?"

"John manages the feed store."

"Is he married?"

"Nope."

His mind wandered back to their dinner at Randall and Barb's. "You were great around your brother's kids. It's obvious they like you to visit."

"I try to spend Sunday evenings with them."

He had never been around kids at all. Although Shaye's mother had died, she knew a lot about being a mother from a practical standpoint.

Veering off that track, he suddenly wanted to know more. "How did you survive growing up with a house full of males?"

She laughed, a soft musical sound that seemed to ripple through him. "It wasn't easy. I often felt as if I were on an alien planet. But I have two really good friends who I've known since grade school. They were my 'sisters.' Once all of us started riding bikes, we could get to each other's places. I had plenty of girl-time with them."

"The three of you are still friends?"

"I don't know what I'd do without them. When I got the call about Julia... They both stayed with me the first day until I finally shooed them off. Gwen, Kylie and I have been through a lot. We're always there for each other."

Shaye's life was hard for Dylan to fathom. She had lots of family and close friends. He had friends, but they were colleagues, not anyone he'd turn to in times of trouble.

Tomorrow he'd have to tend to Julia's memorial service, contact Will Grayson's widowed mother to find out if she wanted to have the service separately or together.

After a considering moment, he asked Shaye, "Was Julia happy?"

Shaye's voice was gentle. "Yes, she was happy. Couldn't you tell?"

"The last couple of years, I didn't know if she was just putting on her party face when I was in town. She seemed happy when she e-mailed me. She told me about everything she and Will did together when they weren't working. Was that real or was she just filling the screen so I'd have something to read?"

"It was real. She and Will liked being together and I rarely saw them apart. When Will found out she was pregnant, he brought home balloons and a teddy bear that was almost as tall as Julia was. They were very happy, Dylan. Never doubt that."

The week ahead loomed like a dark specter. "I'm going to have to go through her things."

"Yes, you are. It might be easier to pack them up and put them in storage, then wait a few months till you actually sort them. When my mom died, my dad left her things alone for months. Then slowly, my brothers and I would see a carton go to Goodwill...a few weeks later, another one. Everyone deals with grief in his or her own way."

Dylan remembered the nights he'd spent in foster care after their parents had died, when he'd been separated from Julia. He hadn't been able to cry. His eyes had stung, his body had felt heavy with a monumental weight. After a few zombie-like days, he'd begun planning how he would see his sister again, how he would make a life for the two of them. He'd always been a man of action and that was the hardest part of watching Timmy in the NICU. There was absolutely nothing Dylan could do.

Shaye shifted, her hip brushing his leg. "Sorry," she murmured.

"Don't worry about it," he returned automatically, then finally closed his eyes. If he slept, he could escape everything for a few hours.

When he awakened, he'd know what to do.

Six hours later Dylan knew he'd slept in the deep, dreamless world he needed. Glancing at the window, he saw the barest hint of light in the gray sky.

Unable to help himself, his gaze fell on Shaye. She hadn't moved much, either. Her face was turned toward the back of the sofa, her hair spreading out over the pillow. His fingers suddenly itched to touch it.

Not wanting those yearnings to start all over again, he lowered his feet to the floor.

Coming awake, Shaye hiked herself up on her elbows until she was sitting against the arm of the sofa.

"I didn't mean to wake you." He studied his watch, the hands visible under the light of the lamp that had burned all night.

"I should find one of the nurses and see how Timmy's doing."

"They would have come for us if there had been a change."

Running a hand through her hair, Shaye swung her legs to the floor. She was close enough that their knees brushed, close enough that his shoulder would graze hers if he leaned a little toward her.

Quickly she ran her fingers through her hair again. "I must look a sight."

"You look fine." Very fine. His body was humming a song he didn't know. He'd wanted to kiss women before but not in this same high-potency, high-need kind of way.

So he didn't touch her. Instead he rubbed his hand over his beard stubble. "I need a shave."

"You shaved last night." Her cheeks reddened because her comment told him she'd noticed.

"If I grew a beard, life would be a lot simpler."

"Do you ever grow a beard?" she asked.

"Sometimes when I'm on a shoot."

Sitting like this, he thought he felt the desire in her to touch him, just as he had a desire to touch her. Should he find out? Maybe if he quelled his curiosity, he wouldn't have such a strong reaction to her. Maybe he wouldn't get aroused every time he breathed her in.

"Do you wear perfume?" he murmured.

Her eyes still on his, she shook her head. "Lotion and powder."

"What's it called?"

"Rose Glory."

He wasn't sure exactly what happened then—if he

reached out to touch her hair or if she leaned into him. The shadowy haze of night, the hush of early morning wrapped around them, creating a world apart. Dylan's hand clasped her shoulder and when he bent his head, she turned her face up to his. There was a bond between them that had to do with Julia and Timmy and everything they'd both lost. But there was something else, too… electricity that only had to do with the two of them. It zipped and sizzled now as his lips neared hers, as he noticed her wide-eyed look of longing, as he thought about what kissing a woman like Shaye would mean.

Kissing a woman like Shaye. He must be out of his mind!

Dropping his hand *away* from her and raising his head, he knew he had to give an explanation. "We don't want to start something we can't finish."

Looking startled, it took her a moment to grasp the meaning of his words. Then she blinked and rose to her feet. "There's nothing to start. There's nothing to finish. I'm going to see if Timmy's doctor came into the hospital yet."

Before Dylan could agree that that was a good idea, she hurried out the door and down the hall.

Standing, Dylan decided not to go after her. He'd get them some black coffee instead so they'd be ready for whatever came next.

Chapter Three

When Dylan came into the NICU Saturday morning, Shaye's pulse raced.

He was later than usual this morning. Most days he arrived about 8:00 a.m. Already it was midmorning.

"How is he?" Dylan asked. Those were usually his first words to her, sometimes his only words.

"Dr. Carrera seems pleased with the lab results."

Dylan's appearance was stark against all the white of the hospital. He wore a black turtleneck today with black jeans and boots. Although she was trying not to react to his presence, her heart sped faster and a cogent excitement she'd never experienced before seemed to fill her body...especially when he came closer and stood at the foot of Timmy's bed.

This week had taken its toll on Dylan. There were more lines etched beside his eyes and his mouth, a weariness that had more to do with grief than with fatigue. They'd been avoiding each other ever since he'd almost kissed her, wandering to other parts of the hospital rather than being in the waiting room together. Most of all, they definitely hadn't spent another night in the same vicinity.

Yesterday at Julia and Will's memorial, Shaye's heart had broken for Dylan as he'd endured the service. She'd watched as he'd said goodbye to Will's mother who was returning to Nebraska that evening. He'd been stoic but she'd known how he hurt inside because she hurt, too.

Shaye rose to her feet.

Before she turned away, Dylan caught her arm. "You don't have to go."

His fingers seemed to scorch through her blouse. The sensation shook her. She knew better than to get involved with a man like him, a man who was here one day and gone the next.

After he dropped his hand, however, she didn't move. Something about Dylan today was pulling her toward him rather than urging her to run away.

"I scattered Julia's ashes this morning." His anguish was mirrored in his eyes.

"Where?" she asked gently.

"She had a favorite spot on Bear Ridge, about a mile south of town. We hiked there, had picnics, just sat and talked. That's where she told me she was pregnant." Shoving his hands into his pockets, he went on, "I couldn't just bury the ashes. I wanted her to be in a place she loved. Do you know what I mean?"

Shaye's chest was so tight she could hardly breathe. "I know exactly what you mean." Reaching out, she touched *his* arm this time. "I know doing that had to be hard for you."

When he looked away, she saw his throat work and she wished they were alone somewhere, alone where they could really talk.

Dr. Carrera entered the NICU and saw them. Chart in hand, he checked the monitors and the readouts around Timmy. "I have good news. I'm going to take Timmy off the ventilator, but I want the two of you out of here. I'll send someone to the waiting room to let you know when you can come back in."

If Timmy could breathe on his own, Shaye just knew everything would be all right.

"Go on, now," the doctor said with a smile. "Go get some breakfast or lunch."

"Coffee would be good," Dylan agreed, his gaze on his nephew, worry etching his brows. Then he turned and headed into the hall.

"If we go to the cafeteria for coffee rather than getting it from the vending machine," he said over his shoulder, his voice rough, "it might taste like more than colored water."

Shaye followed him, feeling his turmoil and his hope.

As they passed the nurses' desk, one of the nurses looked up. "Mr. Malloy, we had a message for you." She handed him a slip of paper. "He said he couldn't reach you on your cell phone."

After scanning it, he told Shaye, "Since I can't use my cell phone in the hospital, I have to find a pay phone and make a call. Go ahead to the cafeteria. I'll meet you there."

In a way, Shaye was relieved to be going to the cafeteria on her own. She felt such a tugging toward Dylan that she needed a reserve of energy to resist it. Over the past few days she couldn't help imagining what a kiss of his would be like and she couldn't keep from picturing what might have happened if he hadn't pulled away.

Nothing would have happened, she told herself now.

She'd never indulged in quick affairs. She hadn't slept with a man since Chad had broken up with her her...since she'd learned his grant in India was more important than she was...that his career didn't include dragging a wife everywhere he went. He'd pulled the proverbial wool over her eyes and she'd felt like a fool. Sure, she'd tried dating. No man had lit an inner fire. No man had tempted her to give up her life as she knew it. At twenty-nine, she realized she was as set in her ways as any woman her age.

When she entered the cafeteria, she headed toward the beverage area. A few minutes later she was sitting at a table, staring into a cup of coffee when a cheery voice said, "Only *one* cup if you don't put any food in your stomach."

The sound of Gwen Langworthy's voice always made Shaye smile. Looking up into her friend's beautiful dark brown eyes, she asked, "What are *you* doing here on a Saturday?"

"One of my patients delivered her baby this morning. I stopped in the NICU to see if you were there but the nurse told me you'd come down here. Are you okay?"

"Timmy's coming off the ventilator. I'm fine."

Gwen was a nurse practitioner, specializing in obstetrics. "Off the vent! That's great. You'll be taking him home soon."

Both Gwen and Kylie had called Shaye often over the past week, offering their support and their presence if she wanted it. Usually Shaye loved spending time with her friends but between her visits to Timmy and the turmoil Dylan caused, she had just wanted to try to sort it all out on her own.

"I hope so," she breathed fervently.

Pushing her mop of curly dark auburn hair away from her face, Gwen asked, "You don't think Julia's brother's going to contest custody, do you?"

"I don't think so, but he—" She stopped because at that moment Dylan walked into the cafeteria.

When he saw the two of them, he gave a slight wave to Shaye and went to buy coffee of his own.

As he was paying for it, Shaye said, "That's Dylan Malloy."

Gwen's eyebrows arched and she looked at Shaye curiously. "Is *he* the reason you haven't wanted us around this past week?"

"I always want you around," she protested. "I just had things to sort out."

Gwen put up her hand to stop her excuse. "I was kidding." She took another look at Dylan. "But now I'm wondering if he doesn't have something to do with those things you were sorting out."

"Don't be ridiculous! You know what he does for a living."

"Yes, but I can also see he has enough sex appeal to stoke the fantasies of every woman in Wild Horse Junction."

As Dylan came toward them, Shaye knew Gwen was right. There was something very sensual about Dylan in the way he moved, in the way he talked *and* in the way he looked at her.

While he approached them, Shaye felt all her senses come alive in a way they didn't when he wasn't around. "Dylan, this is Gwen Langworthy. We've been friends since we were kids."

"It's good to meet you," Dylan acknowledged, extending his hand to Gwen.

She shook it quickly. "It's good to meet you, too. I'm sorry about Julia."

"Thank you. If I'm interrupting…" he started.

"Oh, no," Gwen assured him. "I have to be going. I just wanted to check in on Shaye." Leaning down, Gwen gave her a hug. "Take care of yourself," she murmured. "If you need to talk, call."

"I will."

Then, with another smile for them both, Gwen left the cafeteria and Dylan sat in the chair across from Shaye.

Watching him, Shaye noticed Dylan didn't give her friend a second look, which was unusual. Gwen was beautiful with her curly hair, her deep brown eyes, her figure rounded in all the right places. Shaye and Kylie had always admired their friend's attributes. But Gwen played them down. Ever since her fiancé had left her at the altar, Gwen had withdrawn from the dating scene.

"Phone call all taken care of?" she asked.

"Derek, a journalist who was with me on the shoot in Tasmania, left that message at the nurses' desk. My publishing house is moving up the timetable on the book we're working on."

"What were you photographing in Tasmania?"

A smile the likes of which she hadn't seen before brightened Dylan's face. "Gray kangaroos."

"What kind of book are you working on?"

"A coffee-table book of wildlife around the globe— reindeer in Scotland, hippos in Botswana and orangutans in Borneo. We even did some underwater photography for the book."

"You like to take risks," she said, not approving.

"I don't take unnecessary risks. I do like to get as close as I can get to my subjects. It's one of the signature elements in my photos. It's how I keep working."

"Which do you like most—the danger or the travel?" Her question wasn't meant to be a challenge. She was really interested.

"I don't know if I can separate them. As I said, it's not the danger than I crave, it's my interest in my subject that takes me where I need to be."

"I can't believe that you and Julia were so different. She liked being a teacher, going to school every day. That must seem boring to you."

"Julia felt safer with a definite schedule. That came from having our lives torn apart. She liked her day structured from the outside, I just organize mine from the inside. My life seems random but it's not. I know exactly what I'm doing and where I'm going."

As they were talking, Shaye couldn't help but admit that Dylan was a fascinating man. She couldn't begin to understand why she was attracted to him because she knew she shouldn't be. Maybe she reacted to him so strongly because they'd been thrust into a high-crisis situation and bonded because of it.

After a few long swallows of coffee, he suggested, "Maybe we should go back upstairs."

She knew what he was thinking. If they were upstairs, they'd be closer if anything went wrong with Timmy. She was praying nothing would go wrong.

When they returned to the floor where the NICU was located, Shaye greeted the nurses they passed as they walked along the hall.

"You said your father is a cardiologist. Do you run into him much here?" Dylan asked.

"No, just now and then. He's usually in an operating room or consulting. Dad doesn't see Randall much, either, even though they both spend a lot of time here at the hospital. It's just not Dad's way." Shaye wished her father could be more in tune with all of them, but he wasn't and she'd gotten used to that.

In the waiting room, she tried to concentrate on a magazine rather than another conversation with Dylan. However, he paced and she couldn't help but watch him as he did. She couldn't help but picture him in the wild, riding an elephant, camouflaging himself in the brush, hiking where other men wouldn't go.

When they heard footsteps in the hall, Shaye hoped they belonged to Dr. Carrera. The middle-aged neonatologist came into the waiting room with a slight smile on his face. It was the first Shaye had seen since this whole situation had begun.

"How did it go?" she asked, worry sticking in her throat.

"He's breathing on his own."

Dylan moved close to her then, so close their arms brushed. "Can we see him?" he asked.

"For a few minutes. The lab results are promising, too."

Shaye experienced such relief she almost felt dizzy with it. To her surprise, Dylan settled his arm around her shoulders. "Let's go."

The contact felt right and she didn't stop to analyze why.

As they sat with Timmy, they reached to touch him. Sadness gripped Shaye when she thought about Julia and Will never holding their son, never feeding him, never kissing him good-night. Shaye couldn't wait until she could actually hold Timmy in her arms and she wondered if Dylan felt that way, too.

They didn't talk much except to comment on a monitor or readout, but their gazes met often and quiet understanding passed between them. They both had this child's best interests at heart.

When their allotted visiting time was up, they returned to the waiting room again, which had become a second home.

"Are you hungry?" Shaye asked, feeling pangs of hunger for the first time in several days.

"Actually, I am," Dylan responded with a smile as if he were surprised.

"If you'd like to come back to my place, I can make us something to eat. I thought you might like to see where Timmy will be living. All the hours I've been waiting here, I've been planning what I'm going to do with my spare room."

He took a few moments to respond, as if he was coming to grips with her guardianship of his nephew. "Do you have groceries at your place?" he asked. "We could stop on the way."

"Grocery shopping is probably a good idea. We can call the hospital once we get to my town house to make sure everything is still okay."

"Sounds like a plan."

They both drove their cars to the grocery store and Shaye was glad of that. Being cooped up with Dylan inside a vehicle would be altogether too nerve-tingling. However, the trip through the store was almost as bad. They only used one cart, and he pushed it. The sensation of shopping with Dylan should have seemed strange, but somehow it didn't. Their hips bumped as they walked down the canned goods aisle.

When Shaye glanced at Dylan, he was looking at her.

As she moved ahead of the cart, she left him to navigate on his own. But he was always right there beside her. Their hands tangled as they reached for the same apple. Their fingers brushed as they realized they both liked the same kind of salad dressing. When Dylan insisted on loading the grocery bags into his SUV, she helped him, the sleeve of her jacket rubbing against his, his hands coming to within a few inches of her body when he took a bag from her grasp.

Sliding into her car for the drive to her town house was almost a relief, yet a disappointment, too. She was glad Dylan had agreed to go to her place for lunch.

The older streets of Wild Horse Junction were lined with larch and aspen. Pines decorated backyards and towered high over decades-old houses. Shaye, however, lived in a newer section of town where the western Victorian flavor wasn't as prominent. The groupings of duplexes had high-peaked roofs with modern trim. With tan siding and blue shutters, they announced that Wild Horse Junction wasn't just a small Western town, but rather a growing town. Retirees who didn't mind the volatile winters moved here every year. Tourists on vacation who fell in love with the town sometimes relocated whole families into the area. Wild Horse Junction fostered a sense of community and that's what Shaye liked most.

"Nice section of town," Dylan commented as Shaye opened the front door and they went inside.

"I like it. Gwen lives in a ranch house on a street behind this one."

"Is that by design or coincidence?" he asked with a smile.

"By design. She lived with her father for a few years after she got her training, but then decided it would be better for both of them if she was on her own."

That decision hadn't been an easy one for Gwen, Shaye knew. Her father, an alcoholic, had played on her sense of responsibility for years until finally Gwen realized she was enabling him. That was when she'd moved out.

After Dylan set the bags on the table in the kitchen, he scanned the downstairs.

"This is nice," he remarked, his gaze passing over the rust, brown and turquoise Southwestern design on the sofa, the light oak tables, a sculpture of *The End of the Trail,* as well as a landscape painting of the Rocky Mountains above the sofa. All of the colors coordinated, coming together in the braided rug on the floor.

"I have two bedrooms upstairs," she said in a chipper voice that didn't come off quite that way. Talking with Dylan about bedrooms made her heart beat much too fast.

To cover her confusion, she said, "I'm going to call the hospital to make sure Timmy's still doing okay."

With a nod, Dylan slipped off his jacket and hung it around one of the kitchen chairs. She unzipped her parka and arranged it on a chair across from his. Their gazes met and she felt a trembling start inside.

He broke the silence. "I'd better stow away the eggs and milk while you make the call."

They'd decided on grilled ham-and-cheese sandwiches for lunch, along with deli salads. The meal would take about five minutes to prepare.

Crossing to the counter, she picked up the cordless phone and dialed the hospital. When she reached the nurses' desk, Dr. Carrera happened to be there. Apparently from her conversation with the nurse, he realized who was calling and asked to speak to her.

"The nurse said he's stable. That's true, right?" Shaye asked the physician.

"He's stable. By the end of the week, hopefully we'll take out the feeding tube and he can eat on his own, too. Now I want you to stop worrying, Shaye. Relax. Try to find your life again, because as soon as you take this baby home, it's going to change."

"How long do you think that will be?"

"A few weeks. A month. I can't tell you for sure. But to get ready, you have to stay well, get plenty of rest and stop worrying."

Over the past week Shaye had wrapped her professional demeanor around her, the one that stayed in control, took everything in stride, was assertive when she had to be. Now at Dr. Carrera's words, that facade cracked along with her voice when she answered, "I will."

As she set the handset in the base, tears came to her eyes. They spilled over and ran down her cheeks. There was absolutely nothing at all she could do about them.

She felt Dylan come up behind her. She felt his strong, tall body close to her back. His large hand capped her shoulder. "Is Timmy all right?"

"He's fine. It's just…Dr. Carrera told me to relax and stop worrying. Ever since this whole thing started, I've been operating on autopilot and—"

Dylan turned her around, put his palm under her chin and made her look at him. "I know what you mean. I did the same thing. It's habit for me. After my parents died, I had to come up with a plan…not give in to the loss. Julia and I talked about that once. For me, anger took over instead of grief. It didn't go away until I was finally her legal guardian and we were really brother and sister again. Now, losing Julia was awful, but I have to think about Timmy."

"I know, and she would have wanted us to think about Timmy first. You know that as well as I do." Her tears were falling again. "I just know I miss her and I'm still worried—"

When Dylan enfolded Shaye in his arms, she knew he was giving comfort. As he bent his head to hers and kissed her, she knew they were looking for escape and they needed to affirm life. She never expected to get so lost in Dylan...never expected to respond to his kiss as if her life depended on it. Her hands laced in his shaggy hair, loving the feel of it, the coarse texture of it. While his tongue slid into her mouth, his hands pulled her even closer. There was no space between them. The entire length of her body was pressed against him, and she was excited by the maleness of every aspect of him. His chest was hard. His belt buckle pressed into her tummy. And below that...

How long had it been since a man had wanted her? Since she'd wanted a man? How long had it been since she'd felt fully alive as a woman? How long had it been since touching and being touched hadn't seemed important anymore?

Much too long.

Dylan broke away to trail kisses down her neck, and her knees felt weak. As his fingers fumbled with the buttons on her blouse, she pulled his turtleneck from his jeans. She slid her hands underneath onto his bare skin...into the soft chest hair. He groaned, a deep guttural sound that made her wet. Time and place and reason disappeared as they undressed each other in a frenzy of wanting to touch and taste and enjoy.

They were alive and had to prove it. They had lost and wanted to forget it.

After they were both undressed, Dylan pushed grocery bags aside and lifted Shaye onto the table. Its round edge was hard under her knees. Then he slid her forward until her legs went around him and their bodies met. She wanted their joining but he seemed intent on making sure she was more than ready for it. As he kissed her, his calloused hands caressed her breasts.

"I need you," he said as he rubbed his thumb over her nipple.

"I need you, too," she admitted in a rush, never before experiencing this hungry desire that couldn't wait.

When Dylan's hands slid under her bottom and he pressed inside her, a moan broke from her lips. As she held on to him, she knew she'd never forget this union as long as she lived. One streak of pleasure galloped against the next, and the breakneck speed of the race left her breathless. Dylan's skin was slick and so was hers. They glistened, slid, enjoyed every single moment of pleasure. As her climax built, she began an ascent, the air growing thinner, her world expanding into a universe she'd never known. The experience was like standing atop the Painted Peaks gazing at the stars. The wonder of Dylan inside her seemed too big to comprehend. Giving up logic and rational thought, she let herself go, let Dylan take her to a foreign land where everything seemed possible.

Murmuring her name, he gave one faster and longer thrust and they were both calling out, both taking all the pleasure they could get, both alive in the moment.

However, it only took a few moments for cold reality to set in.

She shivered.

Dylan pulled away.

Their gazes met and held as if they were seeing each other for the first time.

"That wasn't me." Absolutely embarrassed by what had happened, she quickly hopped off the table, scooped up her panties and quickly pulled them on. Then she plucked up her blouse, shrugged into it, buttoning it in a hurry.

"Who was it, then?" Dylan asked almost curiously, as if his world hadn't been shaken, as if what had just happened was commonplace for him.

"I don't…I don't sleep around. I don't—"

With him still naked, she couldn't help but notice every inch of him.

"Don't have regrets, Shaye. We both needed that."

"Not have regrets? Dylan, I've only ever made love to one other man in my life! I've never let hormones rule my head. I've never even thought of doing that…of doing *that* on my kitchen table."

Taking her by both arms now, he gazed into her eyes. "We needed to prove we're still alive and to rejoice in that."

Backing away, she said, "It was wrong."

"In my book, it wasn't wrong or right. It just happened."

Not liking the nonchalance of his attitude, she stepped into her slacks, then pulled them up, zippering and buttoning them.

As she tucked her blouse neatly inside, her hands shook. She felt embarrassed, confused and altogether unnerved. "You and I live by different codes. I don't live for the moment. I think about consequences, and I never get involved unless I know the relationship has somewhere to go."

"And that's why you've only slept with one man?" Dylan asked with a quirk of his brow.

Shaye didn't usually swear, but she felt like doing it now. "This was a mistake. Maybe you sleep with a woman after every shoot—"

"I don't." The words were bit out and she could tell he was angry now.

By the time she ran her fingers through her mussed hair, Dylan was dressed, looking dark, dangerous and much too sexy for her well-being.

"I'd better go."

Keeping her shoulders straight, she responded defiantly, "You paid for the groceries. You should stay for lunch."

She hadn't wanted him to pay, but he'd slipped out his wallet and given the cashier money before she'd had a chance to protest.

"I don't think you want to sit at lunch making small talk any more than I do." He pulled his jacket from the chair, put it on and zippered it. "What are the chances you could get pregnant from today?"

That was always a man's basic worry, she guessed,

feeling tears well up again. She blinked them away, mentally calculating her monthly cycle. "I should be safe."

"There are early pregnancy tests. Maybe you could use one before I leave Wild Horse."

And then what? If she was pregnant, he would stay? She doubted that. Dylan Malloy had a life to live and nothing was going to stop him.

He headed for her door, but before he opened it, he added, "I just want you to know, I've never had unprotected sex with a woman before."

Then he was outside…with the door closing behind him.

Never had unprotected sex? He was handsome, sexy and roamed the world. How could she possibly believe that?

A week later, remembering every minute of what had happened in Shaye's town house, Dylan sat in Walter Ludlow's office, Shaye in the chair beside him.

Clearing his throat, Walter straightened his tie. "Since Julia survived her husband, everything of his went to her. However, since she died, all of it, of course, now goes to Timmy. Because Shaye is his legal guardian, she has jurisdiction over it all. However, Julia left particular personal effects to Dylan, and Will left some to his mother. Since she went back to Nebraska, she'd like the things she inherited shipped back there." He took off his glasses and laid them on his desk. "Shaye, you can live in the house if you'd like, rather than sell it."

"I'd prefer to sell it and put the money in a trust fund for Timmy."

With a glance at Shaye, Dylan asked, "Are you sure you don't want to live there? It's bigger than your place."

"No, I'd rather not."

"So, Dylan," Walter drawled, "I need to know what to do with the things Julia left specifically to *you*. I know Shaye entrusted you with the task of sorting through Julia's personal effects."

Dylan didn't hesitate. "I'll put them in storage." He turned once more to Shaye. "Since Timmy's doing so well, I'll be leaving in a few days."

There wasn't one iota of surprise on Shaye's face. "I assumed you'd be leaving soon," she responded stiffly.

Her words bothered him more than he wanted to admit. Before he left Wild Horse Junction, there was something they needed to settle.

While visiting Timmy this past week, he hadn't seen her much. They'd seemed to arrange their schedules so they wouldn't run into each other. One of the nurses had told him Shaye had temporarily gone back to work and stopped in whenever she could. He visited with Timmy during the day, knowing she often spent the evening there. He'd passed his nights sorting through the transparencies in his spare room, thinking about Julia, barely noticing how his work had changed through the years. He and Shaye had exchanged hellos, goodbyes and "he's doing well today," but that was about it. When Walter had called this meeting, Dylan had braced himself to see her in close quarters again...braced himself for the consequences from their intimate tryst.

Glancing down at his notes, Walter concluded, "I think that's all we need to discuss. Dylan, if you'd like to be present when Shaye meets with the real estate agent, I'm sure she wouldn't mind."

"I don't need to be there," he commented. Spending more time than necessary in that house where Julia and Will had expected to live happily ever after would accomplish no purpose.

A few minutes later, while standing in Walter's foyer, Dylan kept his voice low as he asked Shaye, "Did you take a pregnancy test?"

"Yes," she answered tersely. "I'm not pregnant. You can leave with a clear conscience."

Her insinuation and righteous attitude rankled. "We were both there, Shaye. Neither of us considered protection. You can just be grateful we were lucky."

The silence was so dense, he had to cut it. "I told Walter to send me reports on Timmy. I'll make sure he can always contact me."

She didn't respond.

The urge was strong to put his arms around Shaye, to bring her close, to kiss her again. Instead, he thrust the urge aside.

After he opened the door, they stepped outside. Without a word she headed for her car and he climbed into his. They were going their separate ways.

As he switched on the ignition, he thought about Africa and the animals he'd photograph there. In a few days, Wild Horse Junction would again be part of his past. Freedom and his work called to him as it had for years.

Yet now as he accepted the call, he felt reluctant to go. Two stark truths battered his reasons to leave.

Shaye's touch had affected him at core level.

Timmy had Julia's eyes and nose.

His nephew was the only family he had left. If he fought for custody...

But Julia had apparently believed that Timmy needed Shaye as a mother more than he needed a father—Dylan as a father. Dylan needed distance from this situation to see it more clearly.

His life rattled into complete disorder, he shifted gears and pulled away from the curb.

Chapter Four

End of May

Dylan felt as if he were covered in dust. The morning had been dry, hot and windy in this last week of May, and he'd already exposed five rolls of film. He waved to his guide in the Land Rover that he was almost finished.

He'd gotten some fantastic shots of elephants but the satisfaction he used to experience just wasn't there on this stint in Africa. The past few weeks he'd gone back to the basics, using a traditional camera rather than a digital, forgetting about nights spent at his laptop disposing of shots he didn't like. He'd wanted to fan the old flame that used to grow higher and hotter every time he picked up a camera. Yet this trip when he thought of "flames," he pictured him and Shaye in her kitchen. Whenever he let his guard down, whenever he slipped into sleep, he could feel her skin, taste her lips, breathe in her scent. And underneath his memories of Shaye, he could see Timmy's little face.

Suddenly, Dylan's guide was motioning frantically to him. Dylan usually had a sixth sense about the predators he photographed and now he scoped the area, scanning for danger.

A shot rang out! Dylan swore viciously, realizing his guide hadn't been concerned about dangerous wild animals but rather very human poachers.

When a second shot ricocheted through the brush, Dylan flashed back to Walter's last report on Timmy, detailing the baby's progress. He had to see his nephew again. If he died here and now, Timmy would never know what Dylan knew about his mother. He'd never hear the stories Dylan wanted to recount about Julia's tomboy years, her date for the prom, her dreams for her son.

A third shot zinged past Dylan's left ear. Ducking low, he grabbed his tripod and ran. Under the cover of brush he zigzagged toward the Land Rover. No photograph was worth his future with his nephew. Moments later, he opened the door to the vehicle and hurriedly climbed inside, shaken because he could have lost his life…lost an opportunity to see Shaye again…lost the chance to be a dad.

A dad.

When his guide dropped the Land Rover into gear and sped away, Dylan recalled in detail the morning the doctor took Timmy off the ventilator. He thought about watching his nephew grow up.

His nephew.

Had coming to Africa lost its luster because he hadn't made a final decision about Timmy? About raising his own flesh and blood? About becoming a father?

Dylan knew he had to return to Wild Horse Junction before Shaye adopted Timmy…before the chance to be a father zipped by him like one of those bullets.

Whenever Shaye rocked Timmy, she never wanted to let him go. He was such a miracle. The tiny infant who had been connected to tubes and monitors had gained weight and grown. Shaye loved every little finger, every little toe, every little wisp of hair. When he'd come home from the hospital, he'd weighed five pounds. Now he was ten pounds, three ounces and growing bigger each day.

Rocking him in his upstairs bedroom, she always let him sleep in her arms a bit before she laid him in his crib. She loved being a mom.

When the doorbell rang, she wasn't surprised. Kylie and Gwen stopped in often. In fact, the last time Kylie had been here a few days ago, she'd seemed worried about something. Maybe she'd returned today to talk about whatever it was.

After gently placing Timmy in his crib, making sure the baby monitor was adjusted just so, Shaye hurried down the stairs to the front door. When she opened it, so many emotions assaulted her, she could hardly breathe.

Dylan Malloy stood there in a tan shirt and jeans, his

hair looking as if it had recently been cut. His shoulders seemed even broader than she remembered. His green eyes were so intense she couldn't look away. The excitement of seeing him again immediately gave way to a dreadful fear.

Why was he back?

"Dylan, this is a surprise." She tried to keep her voice as natural as possible.

His assessing gaze missed nothing—from her hair pulled back in a ponytail to the embroidery on her jeans.

"Can I come in?"

Her heart was thudding much too fast and she had to admit she was afraid to let him inside, afraid of what she'd feel when he was there, afraid of what this visit meant.

However, she forced herself to say, "Yes, come in. When did you get into town?"

"Last night."

"I see." But she didn't.

As he stepped inside so very close to her, she caught the scent of his aftershave. It was fresh and woodsy and masculine...like every inch of him she too vividly remembered.

"Can I see Timmy?" His voice held a husky note of anticipation.

"He's taking his morning nap." This time her voice trembled a little. Taking a deep breath, she told herself not to get worked up. Dylan was probably between assignments. He would leave again.

"I won't wake him. I just want to look at him. Walter told me how much weight he's gained. He said he'd run into you at the grocery store and Timmy seemed to be doing fine."

She lifted her chin. "He *is* doing fine."

"I need to see him, Shaye."

Instinct told her that Dylan had returned to Wild Horse Junction for a reason other than checking in between assignments. Fear deepened, almost paralyzing her.

Mechanically she responded, "All right, I'll show you to his room."

As Dylan climbed the steps behind Shaye, she was aware of his booted feet quietly hitting each step. She was aware that something was different about him today, but she couldn't put her finger on what it was.

A sense of resolve, maybe?

At the doorway to Timmy's room, she hesitated only briefly before going inside. Dylan came in after her and took it all in in a glance—the pale blue walls, the wallpaper border with frolicking horses, the bedding that matched, the dark chest and dressing table, the crib and the huge stuffed bear Will had bought for his son. As Dylan's gaze fell onto the crib, he stood riveted to the spot. Slowly he advanced toward it and she felt herself holding her breath.

Dylan stared for a long time, reached out his hand once and then pulled it back. Turning toward Shaye, he motioned outside the room.

Once there, he said, "I need to talk to you."

Everything about Dylan today was purposeful, and his words carried a foreboding she was only beginning to understand. Did he want to take Timmy away from her?

Stalling, she asked, "Now?"

"Now."

Swallowing hard, she turned away from him and on wobbly legs went down the stairs.

In the living room, Dylan sat on the couch. She perched on the armchair next to it. To her surprise, even that still seemed too close. When she glanced into the kitchen, she could remember exactly what had happened there. Dylan's gaze veered in that direction for a second, too, and then came back to meet hers.

"Have you started adoption proceedings yet?"

Her dreams for Timmy were huge, her mind filled with scenes of the two of them facing the world together until Timmy could do it on his own. "I have the paperwork in my briefcase."

Dylan's gaze didn't leave hers. "As his legal guardian, you don't need to adopt him."

She didn't like where this was headed. "No, but I want to, and I know that's what Julia would have wanted, too."

"Is it, Shaye?" he returned quickly. "Or deep down in her heart did she really want to leave Timmy to me? Did she want *me* to be his father?"

Shaye tried to remain calm, but her chest tightened unbearably. "That's not the way she made out her will."

Dylan cut his hand through the air. "I'm not talking about a will. Julia did what she thought was best for me as well as Timmy, but is that what she *really* wanted?"

Shaye's palms grew clammy. "What are you saying?"

Dylan dropped his hands between his knees, studied them for a moment, then met her eyes again.

"When Walter called me back here in February, I was

in shock. I didn't realize it then, but Julia's death brought back everything that had happened with our parents' accident. With Timmy fighting for his life— I think I was operating on automatic."

There was no doubt in Shaye's mind that everything Dylan was saying was true. She was just surprised he had the courage to admit it. Many men didn't have his insight. What his insight might mean to her future rocked her.

"You spent the last three months thinking about this?" She'd expected Dylan would pour his grief into his work...work to forget.

"Not consciously...at least not at first. While I was working I'd think about Timmy, wonder how he looked, when he'd come home. Then I would receive one of Walter's updates. Through it all I would remember Julia and Will, the years when I worked on the paper and Julia was in high school."

Although she knew she shouldn't be asking the question, she wondered if Dylan had thought about what had happened with *them* or if that had been inconsequential in the scheme of things...if that had been a momentary escape. She couldn't step into her kitchen without remembering how wild she'd felt, how she'd craved Dylan's touch, how she still did.

But the two of them weren't the issue here. Timmy was. "Why did you come back?"

"Something happened ten days ago. I almost got killed by poachers."

Her breath caught in her throat.

"When that happened, my life flashed in front of my

eyes. Not only my life as it had been, but life as it could be. Timmy is my nephew, but he's not just that, he's Julia's legacy."

"Timmy was Julia's legacy to *me*," she broke in.

Dylan sat up straight and ran his hands through his hair. "I know you have legal custody, but, Shaye, Timmy might belong with me."

"Might?"

"I spent the past few days in London clearing my schedule. I came back here to stay for a while and to get to know Timmy and make a decision."

She said the words slowly. "Whether or not you want to be Timmy's dad."

"I know you'll make a good mother, but I have to be certain that I don't want to be Timmy's father."

She'd never in a million years expected this. "You can't be a father with the work you do."

"I don't have answers now, Shaye. I just know I came back to Wild Horse Junction to find them."

"What do you expect from me?" she asked slowly, not at all sure she wanted to hear his answer.

"I'd like you to keep an open mind and an open heart, and let me into Timmy's life for a while in a big way."

"So you can take him away from me?" She knew there were tears in her eyes now, and she tried to blink them away.

"You can shut me out. If you do, I can go the legal route to obtain specified visiting rights. Or…we can try to work through this together."

"You're asking too much."

"I'm asking you to help me to put Timmy first."

If Dylan wanted to be a father as much as she wanted to be a mother... Timmy was his flesh and blood. What right did she have to keep the baby? To make him hers? Yet the thought of giving him up tore her apart.

Dylan stood. "I know I've thrown a lot at you. Think about what I've said. When's the best time to visit Timmy while he's awake. Is he on a schedule?"

"As much as a baby can *be* on a schedule," she murmured. "He usually takes an afternoon nap from about three to five and he's in a good mood for about an hour. After that, he gets fussy."

"Why don't I pick up takeout and bring it over about five. We can talk more then."

Squaring her shoulders, she didn't like the feeling that he was steamrolling her. "Maybe I'll decide to get my own lawyer instead of inviting you to supper."

He didn't seem thrown by her threat. "Maybe you will. If you do, we can talk about that, too."

She really had no choice. "All right, I'll expect you around five."

With Dylan standing, she felt she needed equal footing. Rising, she still had to look up at him. "Do you have any idea of how you've just shaken up my whole world?" she blurted.

"Unfortunately, I do. But I have to be sure about this, Shaye."

He headed for the door. When he got there, he stopped. "Chinese or fried chicken?"

"Chinese," she answered automatically.

"See you at five."

When Dylan closed the door behind him, she sank down into the armchair once more, staring straight ahead. The dream of being a mother had been within her grasp and now Dylan could take it away.

She wouldn't let him.

"Soon he should sleep through the night for you," Gwen reassured Shaye as she nestled Timmy close to her to give him his bottle. Her friend had stopped in to say hi on her way home from work.

"I was only up once with him last night." Shaye glanced at her watch, wondering how much time she had to talk to Gwen before Dylan arrived.

Her friend missed nothing. "Do you have a hot date tonight? You keep looking at your watch. Am I holding you up from doing something?"

"No, it's just—"

When Shaye's doorbell rang, her heart fell to her feet. "It's probably Dylan Malloy," she told Gwen quickly. "He's back in town and I'm afraid…I'm afraid he's going to fight me for custody of Timmy."

"You're not serious!" Her friend looked aghast.

"I am. He stopped in earlier and he's coming back tonight to spend more time with him."

"Do you want me to leave?"

"Just sit tight for a little while."

However, when Shaye opened her door, Dylan didn't stand on her doorstep, but Kylie Warner did.

"Kylie!" She hugged her friend. "What are you doing in town?"

Kylie and her husband Alex ran Saddle Ridge Ranch.

Shaye amended that thought. *Kylie* ran Saddle Ridge Ranch as much as she was allowed to while Alex rode the rodeo circuit and was almost never home. The ranch hadn't made a profit for years but Alex wouldn't let Kylie change anything. He kept telling her the price of cattle would come up again and they'd expand the herd. Instead the herd dwindled year by year, prices went down, taxes went up and Kylie was going to worry her blond hair gray.

Leaning back, Shaye studied her friend. In Shaye's estimation, Kylie was the most beautiful woman she knew. Her straight blond hair hung to her shoulder blades while her cornflower-blue eyes showed her intelligence and her spirit. She was smart and had skipped a grade in school. Petite and slim, she'd always been a tomboy, spending more time with horses than people, always ready to jump on the back of one and take a ride.

Kylie returned Shaye's hug. "Are you busy? I had an errand in town and thought I'd stop in."

"Gwen's here. I'm expecting Dylan Malloy soon."

"He's back in town?" Kylie asked as she went into the living room with Shaye.

Gwen shook her head, her auburn curls flying. "Shaye just dropped a bombshell. Dylan Malloy might want custody of Timmy."

"Oh, Shaye," Kylie said, touching her friend's arm. "What are you going to do?"

Although she usually confided everything to her childhood buddies, she had not told them she'd had sex with Dylan. It was so out of character for her that she hadn't wanted to admit she'd been so foolish. "I'm not sure what I'm going to do. He's coming over to talk. I just can't see it. Unless he gives up his career, I don't understand how he can be a father."

Gwen frowned. "Do you think he's willing to do that?"

"I don't know. Something happened in Africa, and he was almost killed. I think the experience has made him readjust his priorities, at least for the moment. But it might not last."

"You hope it doesn't last?" Kylie asked softly.

Shaye looked down at the baby who had become her son. "I can't give Timmy up. I don't know what I'll do if I have to."

Without words, understanding passed from Gwen and Kylie to Shaye. All three of them wanted to be mothers but fate and circumstance hadn't let that happen yet. Shaye had thought now she'd finally know a life with the joy of a child, but Dylan could snatch that away from her.

"You have to find a lawyer," Gwen advised decisively.

Of the three of them, Gwen was probably the most assertive and proactive, capable of juggling more than one situation at a time. She'd learned to do that because she'd never been able to count on her alcoholic father.

She went on, "You can't let Walter Ludlow handle *your* interests *and* Dylan Malloy's. That won't work if you're going to have a fight on your hands."

"Can you suggest anyone?"

"Arthur Standish is thinking about retiring, but hasn't yet. Maybe you should call him."

Shaye wondered how Kylie knew Standish hadn't retired yet. Why would she need a lawyer? For ranch business? Or were her problems with Alex pushing her to think about leaving Saddle Ridge? Kylie was the most private and guarded of the three of them, and she and Gwen had both learned not to ask questions Kylie wasn't ready to answer.

"I'll think about seeing Standish," Shaye answered. "I'm hoping once Dylan sees how much care a baby needs, he'll forget the whole idea."

Transferring Timmy to her shoulder to burp him, Gwen patted his little back. "Babies are wonderful in theory. Even some *women* don't realize that they take twenty-four-hours-a-day care," Gwen agreed.

"We all know what it's like growing up without a mother. You've got to make Dylan Malloy see how much more you can give Timmy," Kylie added.

"Not all fathers are like ours, though," Shaye responded.

"Be realistic, Shaye," Gwen said practically. "Dylan Malloy's job is worse than your father's, and you never saw *him.*"

"Winning the big prize always consumed *my* dad. That's why my mother divorced him," Kylie added quietly.

"Do you regret not going to Colorado with her?" Gwen asked.

"Not for a minute. Dad and I loved horses and had a bond that Mom and I could never share. Besides, I was old enough when she left to know what it was like to have a mom. Actually, a horse is the reason I came to town."

Glad to let the course of the conversation flow in another direction, Shaye waited for Kylie to explain.

Timmy was dozing on Gwen's shoulder as Kylie stood and crossed to him. "Can I hold him for a little while?"

Her friend handed him over with a wry grin. "Sure."

Taking a seat beside Gwen on the sofa, Kylie studied Timmy's chubby face as she talked. "I'm thinking about adopting a wild mustang. I picked up some papers at the land management office."

"As if you don't have enough chores to do," Shaye said with a laugh. Although Saddle Ridge had a foreman who helped Kylie keep everything going, Dix Pepperdale was getting up in years.

"I know I don't need more chores." Her blue eyes were serious as they met Shaye's. "Or the expense. But I've sold a few of my quilts. I need something to care about and gentling a mustang…well, it's something I've always wanted to do."

"Then go for it," Gwen advised her.

The doorbell rang and Gwen and Kylie looked at Shaye.

"You don't have to run off right away," she told them as she went to the door and opened it.

In June, daylight lasted until nine. The evening sun backlit Dylan. In his polo shirt, casual navy slacks and loafers, she wondered if he'd dressed to portray the image of a common, everyday dad. Dylan Malloy would never become an everyday dad.

He was holding two large bags and said with a smile, "It's still hot."

"Come on in. I have company. Gwen Langworthy and Kylie Warner are here."

At that, he looked taken aback, but then shrugged as if a change in plans meant nothing to him. "There's enough food here for everyone."

There was an awkward moment when she and Dylan

stepped into the living room and Gwen and Kylie studied him.

Gwen broke the silence. "Hello, again."

Dylan nodded to her and Shaye introduced Kylie, watching for Dylan's reaction to her. He didn't seem to have one.

"It's good to meet you. Are you the Kylie Warner from Saddle Ridge Ranch?"

Kylie nodded.

"Your name was mentioned in the *Wild Horse Junction Wrangler* this morning."

"Are you sure it was me?"

"You're married to Alex Warner?"

"Yes," Kylie answered a bit warily.

"There was an article about your husband winning the bullriding competition at a rodeo in Colorado Springs yesterday."

Because she obviously hadn't known, Kylie's cheeks reddened. "I didn't see the paper today," she admitted. "I guess Alex was waiting to tell me when he got home." Looking embarrassed, she brought Timmy to Shaye and handed him over. "I'd better be going. I promised Dix I'd help him groom the horses tonight."

Gwen also rose to her feet. "Yep, I'd better be on my way, too."

With Dylan standing at her elbow, Shaye felt almost panicked. He wasn't touching her, but just having him this close gave her goose bumps. "You could join us for supper," she invited quickly.

"Thanks, but I have errands to run yet tonight and laundry to do," Gwen responded offhandedly. She looked from Dylan to Shaye and her gaze seemed to be sending a message to Shaye. *Stand your ground with him.*

"You don't have to see us out," Kylie assured Shaye, giving her and Timmy a hug, and then Shaye a kiss on the cheek. Gwen did the same.

Seconds later, her two best friends gone, Shaye was left standing in her living room with Dylan, unsure of what to do or to say or to feel.

Dozing for the past few minutes, Timmy began wiggling and let out a cry.

Dylan frowned. "What's wrong?"

She shifted the baby's position and put him on her shoulder, patting his back.

"Could be gas, could be he's restless, could be he just feels like crying."

"How do you know the difference?"

"I don't. But once he gets started, he keeps it up for a while. Come on, if we want to eat, we'd better do it quickly."

By the time they entered the kitchen, Timmy's small cries had turned into much louder ones.

She motioned toward her cupboards. "Dishes are in there, silverware is in the drawer. I have a changing table in the den. I'm going to see if a wet diaper is the problem."

A few minutes later Shaye was back in the kitchen, but Timmy was still crying.

Dylan had set two places. Above Timmy's bawling, he said, "Moo Goo Guy Pan, chicken and snow peas, and beef with broccoli. Take your pick."

"I'd better walk him for a while. You go ahead and eat."

Instead of pulling out a chair as Shaye expected, Dylan crossed to her and stood very close. "Why don't I try to hold him for a while?"

She'd never expected him to offer that. She'd never expected him to jump right in. "Have you ever held a baby before?"

"No, but I did hold a lion cub once. Does that count?"

Unable to tell if he was irritated or amused, she was fascinated by the lighter green sparks in his very dark green eyes. Her heart pounded way too fast and it was suddenly very hot in her kitchen. She remembered Gwen's unspoken message. *Stand your ground with him.*

"I don't know if that counts. I do know you have to support Timmy's head."

"I can do that."

When Shaye still hesitated, he warned her, "You're going to have to give me a little leeway. You're also going to have to give me a chance."

Or he'd sue for designated visiting rights and she'd have very little control of his time with Timmy? The implied threat was there and she didn't miss it.

When Dylan reached for the baby, Shaye knew she had to let go.

Taking Timmy from her shoulder, she held him in the crook of her arm and let Dylan slide his hand close to her body behind the baby. She felt that slide of his hand in every fiber of her being. His aftershave surrounded her as he leaned nearer and she remembered running her hands down his bare back, feeling the heat of his skin and the tautness of his muscles.

As Dylan lifted Timmy away from her, he asked, "What position works best?"

"When he's crying, I try everything. Sometimes walking helps."

Although he was handling Timmy a bit gingerly, Dylan placed the baby at his shoulder, holding him close to his neck. "It's going to be all right, fella." He began to walk around the kitchen, jiggling Timmy a little and patting his diapered bottom. The infant's crying subsided into quieter fussing.

Shaye was reaching for the towel she'd thrown over her shoulder to give it to Dylan when the baby suddenly hiccupped and spit up all over Dylan's shirt.

She waited for an eruption or a string of epithets, a grimace, a quick transfer of Timmy back to her. But Dylan just took the towel from her, tossed it over his shoulder and gave his attention to the baby.

"Didn't go down right that time, huh?" Dylan's gaze was worried when it met Shaye's. "Is he sick?"

"No, that happens with babies. Gas, not burping enough. If you want to clean up, I can see if he'll sit in his carrier for a little bit."

Dylan smiled at her. "Next time I'll know I have to bring an extra shirt. If you have a washing machine, I'll just toss this in while we eat."

The idea of Dylan Malloy, shirtless and bare-chested in her kitchen again, made a swarm of butterflies flutter in Shaye's stomach.

This was going to be one very long evening.

Chapter Five

Shirtless, Dylan stood in Shaye's kitchen, Timmy on his shoulder. Shaye's fingers fumbled with the takeout containers. At least on the pretense of looking at Timmy, she could sneak a peek at Dylan.

"Your friends stop in often?" he asked, pulling out a chair with his foot and lowering himself into it. He might never have held a baby before, but he was doing a darn good job.

"When they have time." She latched on to anything to talk about that wasn't explicitly personal. "Gwen's job keeps her busy. Besides office hours, she does home health care for women who can't get to the center, too."

"And Kylie? It's hard to believe she didn't know her husband won a rodeo event."

Although Kylie didn't talk about her marriage, Shaye and Gwen both knew there were problems—lots of problems—but she wasn't about to discuss one of her best friends with Dylan.

When she was silent, he frowned, patting Timmy's back. "I'm just trying to make conversation, Shaye, not poke into anyone's private life."

Apparently he felt as awkward as she did. Waving at the food on the table, she asked, "Would you like a soda with this? Iced tea? Wine?" The last had been an automatic suggestion and now she wished she hadn't offered it. She certainly wasn't going to have any. She needed all of her wits about her to deal with Dylan.

"Iced tea would be fine. Julia used to brew her own peach tea."

"I use her recipe." Shaye's gaze met his and the bond between them was there again.

"Spreading her ashes seemed like a good idea at the time. Now I kind of wish they were one place where I could go and talk to her."

"You can still talk to her," Shaye suggested softly, understanding Dylan's need.

"I know. Walter told me the house sold in a few weeks."

Sitting in a chair across from Dylan, Shaye kept her gaze away from all that tanned male flesh as she spooned broccoli and beef onto her dish. "A young couple bought it. It's their first house. The proceeds from the sale went into a trust Walter helped me set up for Timmy."

"I stopped at the storage unit yesterday. I just needed to touch something Julia had cherished. I remember the day I gave her the jade elephant. Her face lit up. Everything there carries memories I want to keep alive...for Timmy as well as myself."

The furniture Julia had left her brother hadn't been just ordinary, everyday, sell-it-to-someone-else kind of furniture. There had been a curio cabinet that held all of Dylan's gifts to her from faraway places, mahogany-and-glass bookcases that housed all of her books—many worn volumes she'd read several times—and a fancy desk Dylan had bought Julia for her first apartment. In addition, his sister had bequeathed him a Tiffany light and a table that she and Will had found together in an antique mart.

"I need a house," Dylan remarked offhandedly.

"Are you thinking about buying one?" If he was, his stay here *could* be permanent. Her stomach sank and her heart hurt.

"I have been thinking about it. Even if I don't stay, I need a home base, someplace more permanent than an apartment over a farmhouse."

His gaze went to his nephew on his shoulder, and Shaye saw such a look of tenderness in Dylan's eyes that she wanted to cry. One way or another, he was going to be in his nephew's life.

"You'd better eat," she suggested. "Your food's going to get cold. Timmy looks as if he might be falling asleep. Why don't I lay him in his crib?"

"I can lay him down."

When Dylan stood, she absolutely couldn't ignore his broad, tanned shoulders, his flat stomach, his muscled arms. Any hunger for food she'd had left her, the intensity of a more primal hunger taking its place. The intensity as well as the hunger rattled her.

As Dylan carried Timmy to the portable crib in the living room, she followed protectively, meaning to make sure he handled the baby properly. However, she could easily see Dylan had caught on quickly.

He asked, "On his back or on his stomach?"

"On his back."

Dylan was gentle with the baby, who didn't awaken as he nestled in his crib, his little fist at his mouth.

"It's hard to believe he almost didn't make it," Dylan said. "It's hard to believe he's healthy."

"All of his checkups show that he is. Like most preemies, his development might be a little slower in some areas, but then again, he's shown he's a fighter. There might not be any slowdown at all."

They were standing at the portable crib together, so close that Shaye could feel Dylan's body heat. The hair on his arms was lighter than the hair on his head. His chest hair was darker. She could imagine herself sifting her fingers through that curly hair.

Stop it! she told herself forcefully, but memories of how they'd been together had left an indelible imprint.

When the phone rang, she was grateful. Sinking down onto the sofa, she picked up the cordless from the end table.

Recognizing the caller's voice, she focused on the phone call, trying to forget about Dylan and the effect he had on her.

A few minutes later she *had* forgotten about him because the conversation troubled her. To her surprise, when she ended the call, he was sitting on the sofa about a foot away.

"Work?" he asked. "I thought you were on leave."

"I am, for another few weeks yet. But I've been catching up with my cases. That was Sharon McDonald," she found herself explaining. "She and I work closely together sometimes."

"There's a problem?"

"There are always problems, but this turned into a crisis situation. We'd been keeping a watchful eye on a mother and her five-year-old. We were called in one day when the little girl was found wandering at the other end of town. The mother had fallen asleep and her daughter had gotten out of the apartment by herself."

"Fallen asleep, or something else?" Dylan asked.

"Something else, we think. Probably alcohol. We try to keep families together and there wasn't enough cause to remove the child."

"She was wandering alone at the other end of town!" Dylan looked angry.

"I know. But children are fast. Even when you think they're secure, they're not. So we decided to do home visits for a while."

"And today?"

"A neighbor called in. She heard Jessie crying for a long time. She got the apartment manager to open the door when she couldn't get a rise out of anybody inside. It turns out the mother had left Jessie there by herself all day. No one knows where the mother is."

"What will happen now?"

"Sharon called to tell me they'd placed Jessie with a foster family for now."

Dylan shook his head, and Shaye knew that he was thinking about his experience and his sister's in foster care. "It's a good family, Dylan. I interviewed them myself when they applied to be foster parents. Jessie will be well taken care of."

His eyes were filled with doubts. "Are you so sure about that? Are you so sure the couple doesn't have hidden motives?"

"No hidden motives. They want to have kids and are on an adoption list. But that takes time. Until they can adopt, they're willing to open their house to other children who have no place to go." She couldn't help moving closer to Dylan. "You and Julia never should have been separated."

"You're right about that. I could have looked after her and protected her if I had been with her."

This was definitely one of Dylan's strongest attributes—he was a protector.

When Shaye looked up into his green eyes, she was mesmerized by them. She was mesmerized by him. The air between them sparked with the memory of the two of them together. She'd never been so intrigued by a man, or attracted to one, not in this I-want-to-jump-your-bones kind of way.

When Dylan leaned closer, she knew it was a test. He was trying to see if she would back away. Oh, how she knew she *should* back away. But curiosity, anticipation and sheer excitement were too great lures. His arm went around her and again she realized he was giving her a chance and plenty of time to avoid the kiss. She didn't want to avoid it. She'd longed for it ever since the day they'd made love.

Dylan's lips were as sensually captivating as she remembered. The pressure and warmth of them made her tingle all over. With unhurried mastery, he let the desire build until she opened her mouth, needing more. He gave her so much more. His tongue was hot and rough and adventurous, exploring thoroughly, creating a sensation inside of her that urged her to slip her fingers into his hair. What really made her head spin was his hand on her face, caressing her. His tenderness was so absolutely overwhelming that tears came to her eyes. She'd *never* been kissed like this before.

Moaning, the sound of her pleasure made her realize exactly what was going to happen if they didn't stop. They could be having sex again right here on her couch and that wasn't what she wanted. Well, maybe she wanted it right now, but she didn't want the complication of it or the repercussions of it in the days to come.

Pushing away from him, she took a deep breath, trying to put what had just happened into perspective. She'd practically asked for that kiss and she couldn't fault him for acting on desire she'd felt, too.

After he ran his hand down his face, he just sat there for a few minutes looking straight ahead. "What are you thinking?"

"I wasn't thinking. That's the problem."

A wry smile twisted his lips. "Yeah, I know what you mean. I think I'd better go."

"You should wait until your shirt dries."

"Fortunately I can drive without a shirt."

She knew tonight wouldn't deter him from his reason for being here and she was right, because he asked, "Do you spend most of your time here? With Timmy, I mean."

"Except for going grocery shopping and running a few errands, I do."

"How would you and Timmy like to meet me at Flutes and Drums tomorrow around eleven?"

Flutes and Drums was the name of the art gallery in town. In summer, tourists made it flourish. "Any special reason you want to meet there?"

"I have a meeting at the gallery tomorrow morning around ten. I should be finishing up about eleven. We can go for lunch afterward."

The gallery would be a neutral place. It would definitely be better if he spent time around Timmy that way.

"That sounds good."

At least at Flutes and Drums, she wouldn't feel as overwhelmed by Dylan Malloy. She could concentrate on the beautiful artwork instead.

On occasion, Shaye had wandered into Flutes and Drums to look for a gift or to simply soak in the art. As she stepped into the gallery now, a bell above the door tinkled and low, soft, sweet flute music swelled around her. Stepping inside this space was like stepping into a haven of beauty and talent, history and tradition. As she pushed Timmy's stroller deeper into the room, she saw Dylan standing at a desk, talking to the gallery owner.

With her long black hair and blue eyes, Lily Reynolds was a beautiful woman with Hopi ancestry in her blood. When she'd opened the gallery two years ago, the *Wild Horse Wrangler* had carried a human interest story on her. The gallery owner stood close to Dylan talking to him, and Shaye was surprised at the uneasy feeling that seeing them together gave her. They were sharing an animated discussion and seemed almost familiar.

As she approached, she heard Lily say, "I know someone who can matte and frame your photographs quickly so I can get you into an early July show. It would be wonderful if you could be around for it. But if you can't, your work will sell without you. I always sell anything you give me to display almost instantly. In fact, I have a waiting list."

"You're kidding."

"I'm not. I have patrons who visit Wild Horse on vacation and buy one of your photographs. Then they go back to Pennsylvania or New Hampshire or Texas, and a few months later I get a call. They want to know if I have any more of your work. I never do."

Dylan showed genuine surprise at what the gallery owner had told him. "I've gotten so wrapped up in shooting photos for magazines and books the past couple of years, I haven't thought much about selling them in galleries."

"*My* gallery," she reminded him with a laugh. "Maybe you should think about a whole new marketing process, including framed signed prints. I'd love to be your exclusive outlet."

Because Lily really admired his work? Shaye wondered. Or because she'd like to be around Dylan more and to communicate with him even more intimately? Shaye didn't know where those thoughts had come from, but she realized she was jealous of the rapport these two had.

When had she ever been jealous of anyone?

As Shaye wheeled Timmy closer to the desk, Dylan spotted her over Lily's shoulder and smiled. Thank goodness he had no idea of how fast that smile made her heart race.

If she protected herself, she'd be protecting Timmy. Dylan knew she was attracted to him. She had to be very careful she didn't let him use that attraction to convince her to do anything she didn't want to do. She had to be very careful that their chemistry had no place in her decisions about Timmy.

Now, though, she had to let Dylan be around his nephew. Once he realized what everyday care consisted of, he might not be so eager to be a dad. It was her only hope. But since he'd never been around kids before, it was a realistic one.

He was dressed today in a blue chambray shirt, black jeans and boots. No matter what Dylan wore, he looked entirely too sexy, too handsome and too strong for her peace of mind.

Crouching in front of Timmy, he gave the little boy a wide smile. "Mind if I take him out of there?"

"Not if you're careful." She didn't know where that defensiveness had come from.

His gaze locked to hers. "I was careful yesterday, wasn't I?"

"Yes," she had to admit, feeling as fiercely protective as one of the mother lions Dylan captured with his camera.

The gallery owner was watching the exchange, and Shaye didn't know if she was familiar with their situation or not.

Reaching for a small towel at the side of the stroller, Dylan arranged it on his shoulder first. "I've learned," he joked with a wink.

Yes, he was a fast learner…and not only with Timmy. He'd obviously learned what kind of moves she liked when they kissed. It was obvious he listened for her pleasure and tried to increase it.

The cool gallery air was getting hotter.

As Lily came to join them, Shaye really got nervous.

"He's adorable. What's his name?"

"Timothy Andrew," Shaye filled in.

"After my father," Dylan added, his voice low.

When Lily looked up at Dylan, her wide blue eyes were understanding. "Is there some peace in that?"

"Yes, I suppose there is."

Shaye wasn't going to let their conversation become empathetically intimate. "Timmy has several guardian angels looking out for him," she contributed.

"Do you believe in angels?" Lily asked her.

"I'm not sure I believe in their physical presence in this world, but I do believe the spirit of our loved ones is with us and that spirit whispers to our heart, giving us guidance and direction. At least, it can if we let it."

"Interesting," Lily commented, looking at Shaye thoughtfully. "Dylan was telling me you and he might be sharing joint custody."

Maybe these two were better friends than Shaye imagined. In fact, maybe they were a lot more than friends.

"Nothing's been decided yet."

Obviously feeling the tension that had cropped up, Lily backed away from the subject and extended her hand to Shaye. "I'm Lily Reynolds. I don't think we've formally met."

"I've been in your shop a few times." Showing friendliness she didn't feel, she shook the woman's hand.

"Great. Repeat customers are the best ones. Maybe you can help me convince Dylan that time spent in selecting photographs, matting and framing them would be well worth his time while he's home."

Dylan had lifted Timmy up, was holding him high, staring into his eyes as if that helped communicate with him.

If Dylan did the show, then he'd have even more ties to Wild Horse Junction. "Are you seriously considering it?" Shaye asked him.

Lowering Timmy, he held him to his shoulder once more. "I plan to clean out my files. I could select a few."

"I'm talking about a *show,* Dylan. I want more than a few. More like twenty-five. Believe me. If you select them in the next couple of days, I'll have them framed and ready for the show."

Dylan walked Timmy away from the desk, ambling down an aisle to a grouping on a wall. A few moments later he studied a few sculptures on pedestals. Coming to a decision, he agreed, "All right. Why not? I'm going to be here. But I don't want the show to be strictly a wildlife exhibit. I'd like to include some other photos— more of an all-around collection."

"No problem with that. Can you get the photographs to me by the end of next week?"

"Probably. Or soon after. I'll send some out for processing, but I have a service that's fast."

Because Timmy was getting restless on Dylan's shoulder, Dylan lowered him to the crook of his arm. When that didn't comfort the baby, Dylan glanced at Shaye.

"He's probably getting hungry."

"So am I. Do you want to eat at the Silver Dollar?"

The Silver Dollar was a restaurant with Western atmosphere and good food.

"That's fine."

Dylan was already crouching to put Timmy in his stroller. "Okay, little fella. Not too much longer."

When he stood, Lily was right there and he shook her hand. "Thanks for the opportunity to show my work."

"It's a pleasure," she returned brightly, and Shaye felt jealousy stab her again. Lily Reynolds had intriguing blue eyes as well as exotic beauty.

Yet Dylan didn't hesitate to pull away and come over to Shaye.

Before they walked out of the gallery, he called over his shoulder, "I'll see you next week."

As Dylan sat across from Shaye in the restaurant, he watched her feed Timmy a bottle. She'd been oblivious to the surroundings—brands and lariats on the walls—and to the waitress approaching them as Timmy drank. The look of unconditional love on her face did something to him. When had he ever seen that kind of love?

While the waitress stood there with her tablet, Dylan asked Shaye, "Do you know what you want to order, or do you need more time?"

With a start, she gazed up at the young waitress, then looked sheepish. "Sorry. I…know what I want. Turkey sandwich on toast, coleslaw and cucumber salad."

"Buffalo burger, cheese fries and coleslaw is fine for me," Dylan told the waitress, closing his menu, picking up Shaye's and adding hers to it. He handed them to the waitress. "Iced tea okay?" he asked Shaye.

"That's fine." She smiled at him. "Is that your typical lunch?"

"Actually it's not. But whenever I come back to Wild Horse I have to fill up on the Silver Dollar's buffalo burgers and cheese fries."

So he didn't keep admiring the glossiness of Shaye's hair, the peachy smoothness of her skin, the lovely curve of her lips, he glanced around the restaurant. "They painted the walls and rearranged the pictures while I was gone." The Silver Dollar's assortment of photographs included Gene Autry and Roy Rogers. A shadow box with old playing cards and a sheriff's badge hung on the wall near their table.

"You're observant. I guess that's your business." Settling Timmy on her shoulder, she burped him. "Do you find it strange when you come back and things are rearranged?"

"Sometimes when I come home, I feel as if I've been on a journey in a time machine. I go from here to somewhere in Africa and I step back in time in some of the villages where I shoot. When I return, there's a sameness about Wild Horse Junction that I need in between all the rest. A restaurant might have a new paint job, a new bed-and-breakfast might open, but basically the town stays the same."

"I don't know if that's good or bad," she said with a laugh. "I thought you might say you were bored when you came back here."

"Boredom is a state of mind. I don't bore easily."

If that was true generally speaking, she wondered why he traveled around the globe. Julia had told Shaye more than once that she wished Dylan could find a woman with a wandering spirit like his, who was interested in the same kind of work. They could partner up and roam together. As it was, he might have an affair for a few weeks on a location, but when he moved on, the relationship was over.

"Do you know Lily Reynolds very well?" Shaye asked, thinking some affairs might occur over and over.

"I've known her since she returned to Wild Horse and opened the gallery. But that's not what you meant, is it?"

In spite of herself, Shaye felt her cheeks flush. After rearranging Timmy for another burp, she plunked his bottle on the table. "I didn't mean anything in particular."

"Don't lie to me, Shaye." His deep husky voice brought her gaze to his. "You don't do it very well."

Unfortunately she was an open book. When she cared about her cases, she wore her heart on her sleeve. Could he actually see how deeply attracted she was to him? How fearful she was that he was going to take away her opportunity to be a mom…to love Timmy the way she'd always wanted to love a child?

Patting Timmy's back, she tried to be nonchalant. "You seemed to have a rapport. I just wondered."

As he settled back in his chair, he picked up his fork, then laid it down again. "That's what happens with women," he complained. "They talk to each other. I suppose my sister gave you book and verse on my lifestyle, or my lifestyle as she saw it?"

"We were good friends."

When he leaned forward, his eyes were riveted to hers. "No one knows exactly how someone else's life feels until they walk in their shoes…or boots…or moccasins. Julia saw the surface of my life, not what was deep down in it."

"She only knew what you told her."

"Not exactly. She got an impression from what I told her."

"Are you saying you don't live the life of a carefree, wandering bachelor?"

Lowering his voice to plunge them into an intimate conversation, his gaze didn't waver from hers. "I don't have a belt with notches on it. Just like any other man, I like company sometimes. But I'm selective and would rather be alone than with the wrong person."

"How do you know if it's the wrong person or the right person if it doesn't last?"

"If I'd been with the right person, it would have lasted."

His answer might be logical, but in her estimation that logic didn't work. "How can you possibly know that when you don't stay in one place long enough to build a relationship?"

Crossing his arms on the table, there was an edge to

his voice when he asked, "I suppose these are all questions you're concerned about for Timmy's sake?"

"Not only for Timmy's sake." She leaned closer and whispered, "You and I had unprotected sex."

Moments before she could read the emotions in his eyes. Now she couldn't.

"I told you before, I've never had unprotected sex with a woman. I get tested regularly because of the traveling I do. So you're safe, Shaye."

She hadn't known whether to believe him or not when he'd said he'd never before had unprotected sex. Why with her? Maybe the intensity of her attraction to Dylan *wasn't* one-sided. Maybe the feelings for him she'd tried to deny weren't one-sided, either.

More people were filing into the restaurant now and she felt self-conscious having this conversation here. But she went ahead anyway. "Were you as caught up in the moment as I was? Why didn't one of us stop?"

"Because we needed each other, Shaye, and that day nothing else was more important than that."

Need. Desire. Passion. Did they have anything to build on? Should she even consider it?

Timmy began to squirm in her arms. Standing, Dylan came around to her side of the table and held out his hands. "I'll take him for a while."

Then Timmy was in Dylan's arms and Shaye's were empty. She *couldn't* get involved with Dylan Malloy. She couldn't let him take away her baby.

Somehow she had to convince him that Timmy was better off with her and he should go back to the life he loved.

Chapter Six

"What happens after lunch?" Dylan asked when they'd finished their meal.

Not knowing exactly what Dylan was talking about, she felt flustered and grasped for an easy answer. "I'll take Timmy home. We might play with a rattle for a bit or turn on his mobile with the music and the lights. Then he'll take a nap."

As Dylan frowned, she asked, "What?"

"I want to *do* something with him. I want to *learn* to do something with him. Do you know what I mean?"

"He can't play baseball yet," she said jokingly. "His pitching arm isn't quite strong enough."

When Dylan rolled his eyes, she had to smile. "Life's

pretty simple for Timmy these days. He eats, he sleeps, he gets changed, I give him a bath—"

"There we go," Dylan announced, leaning back in his chair. "A bath. I could do that."

She wasn't so sure he could. Wet and soapy babies were slippery. There was a definite art to bathtime until the babies could sit up by themselves. "It's not as easy as it might seem."

"*You* do it."

"I've had practice."

"So let me practice."

She frowned at him, not knowing how to *not* sound confrontational.

Before she could come up with a tactful response, Dylan leaned forward again, hands on the table, his eyes boring into hers. "I'm going to learn to take care of him, whether I sue for custody or not. He'll spend time with me. Don't block my ability to learn."

Quiet anger ran under the surface of Dylan's words. Well, maybe it wasn't anger, just a pure determination to do absolutely everything he could for his nephew.

"I like to bathe him in the evenings," she admitted. "That gives me something soothing to do if he's fussy. A bath seems to settle him down for the night, or at least part of it."

"What time?"

"Between eight and nine, but don't hold me to that. Why don't you bring some of your photographs along."

His brows arched. "Of anything in particular?"

"Nope. I just want to see your work."

After he considered that, he decided, "You can help

me select the ones of Julia you like best. I'll grab a sampling of the others. Are you really interested in what I shoot or are you just making nice?"

His wry tone made her laugh. "I'm interested in what you shoot. Julia told me a few stories and I'd like to see the result of trekking in the wilderness for days or sitting on a mountaintop waiting for the perfect shot."

With a last prolonged look, he said, "I'll be at your place at eight. I know I'm pushing into your life, Shaye, but it's necessary right now."

Necessary for *him.*

She wanted to give him a deadline for how long this could go on or how quickly he had to make a decision about Timmy's custody. Yet she knew she couldn't do that.

What she could do, however, was consult a lawyer. This afternoon she'd call Arthur Standish and make an appointment with the attorney.

When Shaye let Dylan into her town house that evening, he knew she resented his push to be more involved in Timmy's life. Maybe resent wasn't the right word. She *feared* his involvement. From the moment he'd met Shaye, he'd known she was an assertive, determined woman. More importantly, she wanted to be a mother. For those reasons, he couldn't just request she let him spend time with Timmy. Besides, the baby was his flesh and blood and requesting didn't have any part in this.

As she'd suggested, he'd brought his photographs. Although Shaye had insisted she was happy in Wild

Horse Junction, he wondered if that was a defensive position. She'd been willing to travel to India with a man once, but he hadn't asked her to join him. Had she convinced herself Wild Horse Junction would be the center of her universe so she didn't have to take any more risks?

"He's having a pretty good evening," she said as she went toward the portable crib.

Timmy was sitting in a sturdy baby carrier within the crib. A toy on the bars was playing music and flashing multicolored lights.

Dylan stared down at his nephew, not wanting to disturb him when he seemed so satisfied. "How do you know what to buy him?"

"There are several ways to go about it—baby magazines, parent classes, play groups. Stores have more books on the subject than a mother can read. The toy department at our local discount store has a lot of activity toys. The age range is printed on the box."

"Parenthood made easy?"

"I doubt if it's ever easy, but new parents can find help if they want it. The high school offers classes in the fall of the year. My friend Gwen and I were involved in getting them up and running."

"Do mostly women attend?" Dylan lowered his finger to Timmy to see if the baby could grab it.

"Couples sign up, too—more dads each year."

When Timmy caught hold of his finger, Dylan felt so protective toward the baby, his chest tightened. Realizing Shaye was watching him like a hawk, he tried to keep the conversation going to put them both at ease.

"What kinds of topics are covered?"

"Everything from making baby food to disciplining a toddler to dealing with a teenager. The course runs for ten weeks, each session about something different. Gwen teaches a couple of sessions. In fact, she travels around the state helping high schools develop programs for unwed mothers, teaching teachers how to counsel girls who find themselves pregnant."

Keeping his tone conversational while he picked up Timmy, he mentioned, "I bought a few things this afternoon—diapers, a car seat and bottles like you use to feed him."

He cast a glance at Shaye and saw she had gone very still. Dylan cradled Timmy in one arm. "He can come visit anytime."

"I thought you were supposed to be getting ready for your show." She was keeping her tone light but he could hear the worry.

"I was multitasking. While I shopped, I thought about the best photographs to display and the way I wanted to display them."

"I see."

She sounded upset and he wished he didn't have to cause her this turmoil. "Shaye—"

Her doorbell rang and she looked both surprised and relieved.

"Are you expecting company?" he asked.

"No. But it could be one of my brothers. John likes to stop in and eat my leftovers."

"He's the unmarried one?"

Shaye nodded as she went to answer the door.

Tickling Timmy under the chin, thinking he saw a smile, Dylan heard Shaye say, "Dix! This is a surprise."

"Sorry to bother you, Miss Shaye, but I need to talk to you. Do you have a few minutes?"

"Sure, come on in."

After Shaye's guest entered the living room, Dylan studied the man. He was about five foot nine with red hair and a bristly red beard. Holding his Stetson in his hand, he looked to be in his sixties. His plaid shirt appeared new but his jeans had seen many washings.

When he spotted Dylan, he stopped short. "I didn't mean to interrupt. I was in town on an errand. I can come back tomorrow."

Clasping the man's arm in a comforting gesture, Shaye assured him, "Tonight is fine. Dix Pepperdale, this is Dylan Malloy, Timmy's uncle. Dylan, Dix is the foreman at Saddle Ridge Ranch."

Dylan crossed to the man and extended his hand. The foreman shook it. His grip was firm and strong, and as sturdy as he was.

Sensing the cowboy wanted to have a private conversation with Shaye, Dylan nodded toward the kitchen. "I'll take Timmy in there and walk him around the table a few times."

"You can just sit him in his carrier," Shaye suggested.

"And miss private bonding time?" Dylan joked. Then knowing he couldn't ignore Shaye's fears, he assured her, "I'll be careful with him." He wasn't going to ask her to trust him because he knew she didn't.

"All right," she agreed with a sigh.

In the kitchen Dylan had a conversation with his nephew to give Shaye even more privacy, although the conversation wasn't a dialogue but a monologue. "Let me tell you how wonderful your mom was. She loved kids and that's why she taught school. She would have helped you learn rhymes and colors and shapes. Your dad would have taught you all about numbers. They left this world much too soon. But they loved you very much."

The baby looked at him as if he understood every word.

When Shaye came into the kitchen, she took Timmy from him as if she'd been away from the baby all day rather than a few minutes.

"A problem?" Dylan asked since she wasn't volunteering anything.

"I don't know. Dix thinks something's going on with Kylie. She was dizzy today while she was working around the barn. He wouldn't have known except he saw her hanging on to a stall as if the world was spinning. Yesterday morning she was late coming out to the barn and he said she looked really pale. He suggested she go see the doctor, but she insisted it was a flu bug and would pass. He's worried. Not only because she does fifty percent of the chores around Saddle Ridge, but because he's come to look on her as a daughter."

"Where's her husband in all of this?"

"I really shouldn't say anything else."

"It's obvious if he didn't even tell her he'd won a rodeo competition that something's wrong with their marriage."

"Dylan, I really can't talk about it. Gwen, Kylie and I—"

He shook his head in frustration. "I know. The secret club of womanhood."

"No secret club," she responded. "It's called loyalty."

Maybe Shaye wasn't just trying to keep him out of her life. Maybe, unlike some women he'd known, she didn't compete with her friends but was there to support them.

"I'm trying to understand your life," he admitted.

"And I'm afraid to let you anywhere near it."

Although she was holding Timmy, he stepped very close to her. "Why?"

"Because I know how custody battles work."

Now he understood a little better. In her occupation, she would be familiar with tugs of war over children. "I don't want a custody battle."

"No, but you might want Timmy, and I'm not taking any chances."

Tired of their conversation, Timmy screwed up his face and began fussing.

"If we're going to give him a bath, we'd better do it. He'll soon be ready for his bottle," she commented too politely.

Dylan didn't know how to get around Shaye's defenses. He didn't know how to make her understand that he didn't want to hurt her—he just wanted what was best for his nephew.

After they went upstairs, Shaye bustled about nervously, as if she wanted to get this over with...as if having Dylan on her second floor was a crime. Laying

Timmy in his crib, she hurriedly gathered a little wash-cloth and towel, along with a one-piece sleeper with baseballs and bats printed all over it.

"I'm not going to jump you," Dylan assured her.

When she looked at him, it seemed as if she made a conscious effort to relax. "I know you're not."

But they were both remembering what had happened downstairs in the kitchen unexpectedly, hotly, shoot-to-the-moon fantastically. At least *he'd* had a good time.

Had Shaye?

Good time or not, Shaye wasn't going to let it happen again, and neither was he. Maybe she just needed that re-assurance. "Can you simply look at the time I spend with Timmy as an opportunity for you to share responsibility?"

"I don't want to share responsibility," she stub-bornly declared.

With a sigh, he shook his head. "Fine. Just tell me what I need to do." He knew his voice was gruff. He knew he was pushing her. But damn it, he was going to bond with Timmy whether she wanted him to or not.

Turning her back on him, she went to the crib and began to undress Timmy. "You can fill the tub." She pointed to a vinyl one on the floor by the chest. "Put about a half inch of water in it. That slanted seat keeps him out of the water. You want the water just a little bit warm— Maybe I should do it."

This time his voice grew louder. "For goodness' sake, Shaye. I'll be able to tell if the water's too cold or too hot."

"Sorry," she murmured, glancing over at him. "But my water's really hot and you have to test it."

He picked up the tub. "Message received. I'll test it."

After he went to the bathroom, he ran the water until it was just the right temperature then slipped the tub under it. He didn't know why he was losing patience with Shaye. Waiting for the perfect photograph, he could sit in a tree stand for hours. But this woman pushed his buttons.

Because he was attracted to her?

He'd been attracted to women before yet had never felt this disturbed restlessness he experienced around Shaye.

Once more in Timmy's room, he set the tub atop the vinyl pad on the chest. "Is this where you want it?"

"Yes, that's fine. I wash his hair when I give him a bath. Do you want to take care of that, too?"

"Sure. Just show me what you use."

Squiggly now, Timmy fussed and seemed to be revving up to a full-blown cry. "I guess you usually try to do this quickly?"

"That depends on his mood," Shaye confided with a small smile that was a little bit mischievous. He had a feeling she was glad Timmy wasn't in a docile frame of mind.

Using his hand, Dylan dribbled water over Timmy's head, trying not to let it run down his face. The baby quieted. In a matter of minutes, Dylan had shampoo in one hand and was holding Timmy steady with the other. He shampooed the baby and took the soap Shaye offered so he could do the rest of his little body. Timmy seemed to be enjoying it.

"How long until he can sit up on his own?"

"At about six months, unless it takes him a little longer."

As Dylan soaped Timmy and held him so he didn't slip down the incline, he mumbled, "I need four hands."

"That's why bathing a baby is an art." When he cast a sideways glance at Shaye, she was smiling and he could tell she was attempting to lighten up a little.

When he'd started bathing Timmy, Shaye had put a plastic cup in the tub. Dylan used it to rinse the baby off. When she handed him a towel, he said, "Next time I'll have to throw that over my shoulder, then I'll be ready. I can see why taking care of kids takes planning."

"You're a fast learner." Her voice was filled with grudging admiration.

"I've had to be a fast learner all my life. I imagine you had to be, too." He thought of living with her father and two brothers after her mother died.

"I guess we learned fast to survive." She was lumping them together and he felt good about that.

Carefully, he lifted Timmy from the little incline with the towel, taking him over to the crib. The baby looked at him wide-eyed with his little fist pumping back and forth, then let out a howl.

"What's this about?" he asked the infant above the cry.

"He's getting hungry. Do you want to dress him or warm up his bottle?"

"I'll dress him." When she was still standing there a few moments later, he said, "I know you want to do this yourself, and if not that, you want to watch every move I make. I will *not* hurt him."

She worried her lower lip and finally admitted, "I've watched young mothers with newborns. They don't have a clue as to the first thing to do. Everyone seems to think parenthood comes naturally, and it doesn't."

After he finished drying Timmy off, he knew he had to get a diaper on him before anything else happened. Reaching for the diaper, he quickly took the paper from the tabs and attached it as if he'd been doing it for a lifetime. It wasn't a snug fit and Shaye probably could have done a better job, but it was adequate for the first try. She must have thought so, too, because she left the room and went downstairs.

When Shaye left Dylan alone with Timmy, she just wanted to cry. He was acting like a real dad. It wouldn't take him long to pick up whatever he had to learn. Then he wouldn't need her. He and Timmy would be fine on their own. That picture was too painful to examine.

Downstairs in the living room she could hear Dylan on the baby monitor talking to his nephew as if the baby could understand.

"You've got to eat so you get big and strong…burping will help your digestion…when you sleep, I wonder what you dream." She almost felt as if she should turn the monitor off because it seemed Dylan had forgotten it was there.

She took a bottle upstairs to Dylan and waited while he started feeding Timmy, realizing she couldn't watch over him every minute. Dylan confirmed that when he said, "Go downstairs, Shaye. We'll be fine."

Reluctantly going to her first floor, not knowing what

else to do, Shaye made a batch of iced tea. Meanwhile she tried to get her emotions under control. She felt terrible for just wanting Dylan to go away again…at least part of her wanted him to go away for more than one reason. She wanted to be Timmy's mother. Fighting her attraction to Dylan was becoming more difficult, too. She'd made an appointment with Arthur Standish for next week but didn't know what would come of it. After all, Timmy was Dylan's nephew. Even if she remained the baby's legal guardian, Dylan had a right to time with Timmy.

When Dylan came downstairs and into the kitchen, he was smiling. "Timmy is fed, burped and on his back. I think he fell asleep as soon as I laid him down."

"He slept five hours straight last night." She motioned to the tea. "Would you like a glass?"

"Sure."

"It's herbal," she said to make conversation, "so you don't have to worry about it keeping you up."

"I'm going to be up tonight, anyway. I have to make decisions about the transparencies I want processed. I have to play with a few other photos on the computer."

Dylan had laid a leather portfolio case on the table. "Are you still interested in these?"

Shaye had seen a few of Dylan's photographs in magazines, but she wanted to see more and to learn who he really was as an artist. Photography was an art, just like painting or sculpting. She had a feeling if she examined his photographs, she'd see the world through his eyes. It was an intriguing concept.

"Yes, I'd like very much to look at them."

Be polite...be friendly...don't give away how worried you are about Timmy and your attraction to his uncle.

Almost immediately Shaye realized she had to sit side by side with Dylan so he could explain the photographs. Maybe this wasn't such a good idea. Pulling out a chair and taking a seat, she maintained a good six-inch distance between them. He didn't seem to notice as he unzipped the portfolio and sat beside her.

Suddenly six inches wasn't nearly enough. Every time she breathed, she could easily catch whiffs of a woodsy aftershave. She was close enough to see the tiny nick on his jawline where he'd cut himself shaving and to feel the heat that was male and pulling her toward him. It was almost a physical feat for her to stay away.

As he turned over photo after photo, Julia smiled up at Shaye. At least, in most of the photographs she was smiling. There was Julia with binoculars on a craggy rock looking into the distance. Julia by a stream, jeans rolled up, dipping in one big toe. A younger Julia, silent, pensive, sitting in a park, lost in a world of her own. There were pictures of Julia swinging and trying to touch the clouds with her toes, doing the two-step at a square dance with Will's arm around her. In the last one Julia was holding a kitten to her cheek.

"I wish I had shot one of her pregnant," Dylan said with regret.

"She did have that glow pregnant women get. Everyone looking at her knew she considered herself the happiest woman in Wild Horse Junction, or maybe the whole wide world."

"Do you ever ask yourself the whys?" Dylan's eyes were filled with doubts and pain and questions that he couldn't find the answers to.

"Sure, I ask why. As soon as I lost my mom it was the big question no one could answer for me. But I soon found out I shouldn't waste my time on it, because I wouldn't ever know the answer."

"I know that, but I still ask."

Had asking why brought him back to Wild Horse Junction to consider being a father? She didn't want to get into that conversation again. The tension between them seemed to have diminished, but his shoulder was awfully close to hers. Their hands were almost touching above the photographs spread on the table. She pulled her hand back and put it in her lap.

"How many are you going to choose?"

"I'm not sure yet. Which ones do you like?"

Easily, Shaye pointed to the toe-dipping, the kitten and square dance photos. "I like these the best."

Nodding, Dylan shuffled them all into a pile again, put them aside and picked up the manila folder with the eight-by-ten photos.

"These were all taken in Africa."

Dylan's talent shouted at her as she examined each photo—giraffes running across the plains like a large orange wave, a leopard climbing a rock at dusk, a mother lioness protecting her cubs, elephants at a watering hole. There was scenery, too, and she got lost in the beauty of it, almost feeling as if she were there.

Obviously, Dylan saw a magnificent world and she

had no doubt that he wanted to share that world with Timmy.

"I can see why the gallery sells out of your work. You don't just take a picture, you paint a portrait with light, shadows and color."

"Thank you. Not everyone can understand what this is all about."

"It's about you telling a story in a single frame."

"Exactly." Somehow they leaned closer. Somehow their breaths mingled. Somehow...

His lips covered hers and she instantaneously responded. When his hand went to her neck and slid under her hair, she sighed, opening her mouth, letting him in. As before, her heart raced, she trembled and then she pulled away.

"I can't kiss you," she murmured.

"You *were* kissing me."

Using the table as a prop in case her knees weren't quite steady, she pushed herself up.

He caught her arm. "You can't live in denial about the attraction between us. We're going to see each other often because of Timmy."

"I can't get involved with you when you might sue me for custody of the baby I've wanted for years!"

Silence seemed to ricochet off the kitchen walls and then Dylan was gathering up photographs, sliding them into the portfolio and zipping it. "It's not that cut and dried, Shaye."

Her phone rang and she reached for it, thankful for the interruption. "Hello?"

"Shaye, it's Kylie."

Her attention immediately focused on her friend. Remembering what Dix had told her, she kept her voice light. "Hi. What are you up to?"

Dylan lifted his portfolio from the table and said, "I'll be in touch," and then left her kitchen and her town house.

"Shaye? Is someone there with you?"

"Not anymore."

"Dylan Malloy?"

"Yes, but he left."

"Why was he there?"

"To give Timmy a bath and put him to bed."

"Shaye—"

"It's okay. I'll get it sorted out. What about you?"

"That's why I'm calling. Can you come over tomorrow afternoon? I'd stop by your place but I have an appointment early in the morning and then I have to be back here. The vet's coming to check the horses."

"Is something wrong with them?"

"No, just his annual visit. But I need to be here because Dix and Alex won't be."

She knew better than to ask about Alex. "Where will Dix be?"

"Something's wrong with my truck and he needs to take it to the mechanic."

"What time do you want me?"

"Come over about one. I'll have lunch for us."

Protesting that Kylie didn't have to go to that trouble would do no good. "Is it okay if I bring Timmy?"

"Of course, it is. You don't even have to ask."

Shaye hung up the phone. Although she was upset about Dylan, she was also worried about her friend.

Was Kylie sick?

Shaye knew she'd be counting the minutes until she found out.

Chapter Seven

As Shaye drove into the sloping valley, she was struck by the beauty of the mountains against the blue sky, the green of the grazing fields, the pines and maples and oaks that had grown on Saddle Ridge for decades. Years ago, the ranch had been an equine center of high repute. Kylie's father-in-law had been a renowned trainer and breeder of championship cutting horses. After her dad died her last year of high school, Kylie had gone to work at Saddle Ridge as a trainer. Then Jack Warner's heart problems had slowed him down and his son Alex had taken over management. Management was the problem with the ranch now. Kylie knew exactly what to do with the horses, but Alex Warner hadn't been good at nourishing his father's legacy.

Glancing at Timmy in the back seat, Shaye saw that he was awake but content, at least for the moment. As she passed the split-rail fence that needed repair, she remembered what Saddle Ridge had once been and realized Kylie was wearing herself out trying to handle everything alongside Dix, including training clients' mounts and digging fence posts. Experienced at ranch life, she knew what had to be done. But there simply weren't enough hours in the day to do it, not when there was livestock to care for. To Kylie, the horses were more than livestock. If she had to choose between giving the horses the attention they needed and digging fence posts, she'd care for the horses. There weren't many that belonged to Saddle Ridge now. Some of them had had to be sold off, as had many of the cattle.

The old house dated back to the early nineteen hundreds. It was a large two-story structure, modernized with yellow siding and blue-gray shutters. But even refurbished houses needed care. Kylie could unclog a drain and tack up new weather stripping, but the pipes were getting old, the windows let in more air than they should and the wraparound front porch needed a good coat of white paint.

As usual, Kylie was in the barn when Shaye arrived. Apparently hearing the car on the gravel parking area, she exited the side door of the huge red barn and waved. There was a pickup parked near the corral side of the barn and Shaye wondered if that belonged to the vet.

When Kylie approached, Shaye could tell she forced a smile onto her face until she saw Timmy and the smile became genuine. "He's awake."

"Yep, but I don't how long contentment's going to last. I brought a bottle. We'll see what happens."

After they walked up the path to the house together and climbed the steps, Kylie took the diaper bag from Shaye and let her friend precede her inside.

"I have beef salad, greens, yogurt and fruit cups. How's that sound?"

"That sounds great. Is the vet here?"

"Yes. If Seth needs me, he'll come get me."

They went through the living room, passing a large plasma-screen TV Alex had bought so he could better study his rodeo technique when he replayed the video-tapes. He'd told Shaye that one day when she'd stopped by and he was actually there.

Shaye knew Kylie had accepted Alex's marriage proposal because they'd grown up together as kids and had been friends. But after his father died, Alex had gone a little wild and had spent money targeted for running the ranch on a state-of-the-art tractor, a custom-made saddle and his own personal mechanical bull. All Alex had ever wanted to do was to compete on the rodeo circuit. Shaye followed her friend into the kitchen, positioning Timmy's carrier on the fifties-style table. Unzipping the diaper bag, she removed the bottle and set it on the top shelf of Kylie's refrigerator.

"Have a seat," Kylie said. "I just have to pull every-thing out of the fridge."

Soon they were seated at the table and Kylie was shaking a rattle at Timmy rather than doing justice to the beef salad on her plate.

Shaye began eating while she watched her friend

closely. "So, what's on your mind?" she finally asked when Kylie seemed oblivious to her perusal.

Kylie's blue eyes were terribly troubled as they met Shaye's. After a deep breath, she confided, "I'm pregnant."

Shaye wasn't sure how to greet the announcement because she didn't know where her friend's marriage stood. "How do you feel about that?"

Her voice soft and warm, Kylie replied, "I love the idea of having a baby."

"But?"

"Alex and I have grown so far apart. He's never here." She shook her head, her eyes misting over.

"Maybe things will change. Have you told him you're pregnant?"

"Not yet. I just had it officially confirmed this morning. I had an appointment with my doctor."

"What are you going to do?"

"I'm not sure. If Alex doesn't make some changes, I might have to leave him."

Shaye knew how difficult leaving would be for her friend. "Where would you go?"

"Not far. I could get a place in town. My computer skills are good because of keeping the books and recording documents on the horses. I spoke with Mr. Tompkins at the temporary agency. There was an ad in the paper that he had a position open. I could interview clients and manage his office. I was looking into the job before I knew I was pregnant. We need to bring more money in and I was going to work away from the ranch."

"And when would you have time for that?" Shaye asked, knowing ranch life was a twenty-four-hours-a-day job, especially with a husband who was *in absentia* most of the time.

"I was waiting for Alex to get home and then I was going to talk to him about it. He has to face the reality of our debts, especially now with the baby."

"It might be easier for you to stay here." Shaye put her thought into words, knowing this was exactly why women didn't leave a bad marriage.

"If Alex won't go to counseling with me, if he won't make some changes, then I have no choice but to leave. I want my baby to have a good future. The rodeo purse Alex won brought in twenty-five thousand dollars, but we have a mortgage in arrears, credit card debt and ongoing expenses that will eat it up."

"You've been thinking about this for a while, haven't you?"

"The past few months. The truth is, I think he's having an affair."

At Shaye's lack of expression, Kylie said, "You don't seem surprised."

Crossing her arms in front of her on the table, she sighed. "I don't know what to say." There had always been rumors about Alex Warner, but Shaye had hoped they weren't true. "Have you confronted him?"

"Oh, yes. I've been getting hang-up calls. The last time he was home, when I washed his shirt, I smelled perfume. He denies it. He always has an explanation. But I think I've been too trusting and gullible. It's time we faced all of it."

"Do you think he'll go for counseling with you?"

"I don't know. I found a male psychologist who counsels couples. I thought Alex might feel more comfortable with a man. Every time I've mentioned it in the past, he's adamantly refused. He says all of my problems are in my head."

"Have you contacted Brock?" Brock was Alex's older half brother. As a child Kylie had adored him.

"No! I would never do that. After what happened with Jack, Brock doesn't want anything to do with Saddle Ridge."

"Brock could talk some sense into Alex."

The shake of Kylie's head was as vehement as her tone. "I don't want to bring Brock into this. When his father willed Saddle Ridge to Alex, that was a slap in the face and proved to him that he never really belonged here."

Reaching across the table, Shaye took her friend's hand. "You know I'll help you any way I can."

"I know. But I don't want to depend on anyone for help. I'd rather figure out my life on my own."

If Kylie had a flaw, that was it. Yet Shaye realized she and Gwen shared that particular flaw, too. They wanted to be independent, self-sufficient women and sometimes that caused more problems than it solved.

Dylan had stayed away from Shaye and Timmy for the past few days for many reasons. First, he knew he was pushing her, maybe too hard and too fast. He wanted to give her a little space and time to think about him being Timmy's father and the idea of sharing joint custody. Second, being around her strained his self-control. In the past, he'd been able to shut a woman out of his thoughts. He couldn't seem to do that with Shaye. Maybe he should spend time with Timmy alone without the distraction of Shaye, without the scent of her rose lotion, the sight of her pretty face, the sound of her quietly steady voice. Engrossed in getting his gallery showing together, he tried to put the rest aside, but he wasn't having a lot of luck at that.

It was almost seven one evening when his cell phone rang. At his computer, he answered it, studying the photos on the monitor.

"Malloy here."

"Dylan, it's Walter."

"Hi, Walter. Do you want to meet me for a late dinner at the Silver Dollar?" His stock of groceries had run out and he was getting hungry.

"Maybe another night. Have you seen Shaye lately?"

"You mean, today?"

"I mean recently. Has she told you her plans?"

"What plans?"

"I don't know precisely but I do know she saw Arthur Standish yesterday."

"Arthur Standish, the attorney?" After a short, startled silence, Dylan asked, "Do you know what she consulted him about?"

"I think it should be obvious what this is about. Custody."

The implications of what Walter was telling Dylan made him go cold inside and then that cold turned to anger. "How do you know about this?"

"We're living in Wild Horse Junction. Somebody sees somebody enter an office somewhere… You know how it is, Dylan."

He knew exactly how it was and didn't know whether to be grateful or frustrated by it. "I'll find out what's going on and get back to you."

"Go easy, Dylan. If Shaye's planning a custody fight, you don't want Timmy to get caught in the middle."

"He's *already* in the middle. Maybe I shouldn't have been so forthright with her. If I'd surprised her—" He knew there was no point in thinking about what-ifs and if-onlys. "I'll get back to you after I talk with her."

Away from his desk now and pacing, he speed-dialed Shaye's home number. Her machine came on. Swearing, he punched in the speed-dial number for her cell phone, and she answered on the third ring.

"Shaye, it's Dylan. We need to talk."

"I can't right now."

He heard voices, lots of them, the sound of a gathering somewhere. "Where are you?"

"That's none of—"

"Shaye, I know you saw a lawyer. Where are you?"

Silence…until eventually she answered. "I'm at the high school at a meeting."

"For work?"

Her hesitation was prolonged until finally she answered, "No. It's a meeting for parents who have adopted or are planning to adopt."

Dylan had never been a reckless man. As soon as he'd gotten control of his life and Julia's, he'd planned every detail. Now he was feeling reckless. "I guess I should attend, too, since I'm also considering adopting Timmy. I'll see you there in ten minutes."

When she didn't answer, he asked, "Is Timmy with you?"

"No, he's with Barb and Randall." A note of fear crept into her voice. "Don't think you can just go over there and take him."

Dylan's anger morphed into something that went much deeper and bothered him greatly. "You think I'd do that? You should know me better than that."

"I don't know you, Dylan. I only know what Julia told me and what I've heard and seen in the past week."

"You're conveniently forgetting the time I spent here in February?"

In the silence, he knew that scenes were replaying in her mind as vividly as they were replaying in his.

"We were in a crisis situation then. Everything was heightened. Nothing was real."

"Our grief over Julia and Will was real. Our fear and concern for Timmy were real. What happened in your kitchen that day was real."

A few moments passed and then she murmured, "I've got to go. The meeting's starting."

"Ten minutes," he reminded her. Then he switched off his phone and headed out the door.

Signs in the lobby pointed Dylan in the right direction. As he walked down a corridor, he could hear voices coming from one of the rooms, people talking and discussing.

When he stopped in the doorway, a moderator

perched on the edge of the desk at the front of the room motioned him inside. Chairs were arranged in a circle so everyone could see each other while they were talking. He really didn't want to pull into that circle, but he saw that Shaye had.

Going around the outside of the grouping, he pulled a chair from near the wall and positioned it behind her. When she would have stood to move her chair over for him to join in, he laid his hand on her arm.

They both froze.

Leaning close, he murmured in her ear, "I'll stay right here." Was that a tremble he felt when he touched her? Was she reacting from fear, from anxiety or from the elemental desire that coursed through him every time he got this close?

During the discussion, Dylan remained silent, listening and absorbing. Couples shared their experiences about adoption—agency adoption, private adoption, adoption waiting for an unwed mother to have her baby. There was some talk about home visits and what social workers might look for. Shaye already knew about all that and he suspected she'd come to this meeting to feel she was moving forward in some way. At least, that's what he hoped. There was no way he was going to let her file for adoption without the case-worker knowing he was in contention for parenthood, too. And he was.

He still hadn't figured out everything about it, but Timmy was his nephew and he wanted him for his son. Not just for Julia's sake, but for his own. He wanted to take him to his first baseball game. He wanted to tuck him in bed on Christmas Eve and watch the wonder in his eyes as he discovered presents under the tree the next morning. He wanted to help with homework and take him to the video arcade. He wanted to be Timmy's dad.

Sitting behind Shaye, Dylan couldn't help but notice the straightness of her spine and shoulders, the tilt of her head when someone spoke and she listened, the scent of roses that, as he inhaled, brought back memories that he shouldn't be having right here, right now.

When the meeting ended, the moderator motioned to a table at the back where a punch bowl and cookies sat. "Help yourselves," she invited with a smile. "I don't want to have to take the cookies home."

If Shaye had been interested in mingling, that was just too bad. He had to find out why she'd gone to the lawyer and what she discussed with him. *If* she'd tell him.

When he nodded toward the door, a stubborn look came into her eyes. "I need something to drink. I'll be right out."

Rebellion, defiance, sheer determination not to give him what he wanted squared her shoulders. They were going to have a rocky road to travel.

When Shaye emerged from the punch and cookie corner, she was holding a cup of punch.

"We can talk in there," Dylan suggested, pointing to an open classroom.

"I have to pick up Timmy."

"Do you want to go to your brother's and discuss this?"

She wouldn't. Having people around wouldn't change his position.

After she took a sip of punch, she peered at him over the rim of her cup and shook her head.

"I'm not trying to corner you, Shaye. If we pick up Timmy, we'll have to see to his needs and we won't get a chance to talk."

"All right," she conceded with a sigh, and went toward the dark classroom.

Reaching it first, Dylan switched on the light. It was bright and glaring. He saw that as a good thing. This had to be a straightforward discussion with no intimate overtones, no chemistry getting in the way of what he needed to say. Maybe that was part of the problem. His chemistry with Shaye had gotten in the way. He hadn't wanted to hurt her or demand too much or push too hard. Now, however, she'd changed all that.

As she sat in the desk in the first aisle, he turned another to face her and lowered himself into it. The kid gloves were off and he wanted answers.

"What did you and Arthur Standish discuss?"

"Is this going to be an interrogation?" she asked with a raised brow. "Because if it is, I'm out of here."

"Do you know how frustrating you can be?" Dylan muttered.

"Because I won't back down or listen to your every word as if it's gospel?"

His voice took on a firm tone. "I never said I had answers, Shaye. I understand full well that Julia made you legal guardian of Timmy and you want to be a mother. But I think Julia did that out of what she saw as necessity. If she'd known I was willing to take Timmy, I don't think there'd be any question of who would have custody of him now."

There was a flicker in Shaye's eyes that told him he'd hit a nerve. "So what did Standish tell you?"

Still she remained silent.

"Maybe I can fill in the details. My guess is, as Walter told *me,* Standish probably told *you* that you have about a sixty-forty chance of retaining custody. After all, you're legal guardian in the will and you're a woman. However, on the forty percent side, I'm the baby's uncle and his family—flesh and blood. The bottom line is, a judge will decide who gets the benefit of the doubt. If we get embroiled in a legal battle over this, we're putting our fate in the hands of a third person—the judge. Is that about right?"

Shaye looked down at her punch cup on the desk, turned it slightly with both hands and didn't look up. "That about covers it."

"So my question to you is, what are you going to do? Do you want to spend time and money in a war? Or do you want to figure out what's best for Timmy if we're both in his life?"

Her chin came up and her eyes sparked. "Now let me ask *you* a question. What kind of life can Timmy have if you travel the world? Children need stability. How can we share joint custody when you'll be gone for months at a time? Your work is your life and you're not afraid to take risks for it. What does that mean for Timmy?"

"More than anyone, I know a child needs stability. I gave that to Julia and I can give it to Timmy."

"But do you *want* to? If you build a life in Wild Horse Junction, aren't you going to resent it?"

"I never resented a minute I took care of Julia."

"That's because you knew you could eventually escape."

Running his hand through his hair, he knew he had to consider her reasoning. "All right, that's true. But if I become a father, I'll have a reason to make changes. In spite of my traveling, I spend a lot of time in London in between. Instead of London, I could make Wild Horse Junction my base. I might be in the field two months and then home three, putting everything together. We'd have to be flexible."

"In other words, every time you come to town, you want me to put Timmy in your arms and say, 'Goodbye for now, honey. I'll pick you up when Dylan leaves again.'"

"It wouldn't be like that. We'd both be in his life. I wouldn't cut you out, even when I'm caring for him. He needs two parents and that's what we can give him. You've got to admit, you're going to need a male role model in his life, and when he gets old enough, I could take him along on some of my shoots."

"No!" The word came out of her mouth like a cannon shot.

Immediately he deflected it. "You're *not* going to overprotect him. That's no way to prepare him for the world."

"I'm going to keep him safe."

"Oh, Shaye," Dylan said with a sigh, sitting back in the desk chair. "Safety is an illusion. You know it and I know it. Of course we'll keep him away from pill bottles and disinfectants and sharp corners as much as we can. But at some point, we won't have control of his world and you know that."

"I won't let him go with you and get anywhere near a lion!"

In spite of himself, Dylan had to smile. "I photograph animals other than lions and you know that, too. I'd never intentionally put him in any danger. Besides, this discussion's a little premature. I wouldn't take him anywhere exotic until he's twelve or thirteen."

"Exotic?"

"Yes, exotic. When I was shooting kangaroos in Tasmania, I have never before seen scenery like I saw there. It's too magnificent to even describe."

Searching his face, she looked for true intent. He knew she didn't trust him to do what was best for Timmy.

"If we did have joint custody, you'd have to get my approval on any trip," she maintained.

He frowned. "Put another way, we'd consult on all decisions."

"You don't give an inch, do you?" she muttered.

"Not when I'm negotiating on something that is very important to me."

He knew he hadn't won her over and her expression was begrudging as she thought about the things he'd said.

"Shaye, you said you don't know me. I understand trust plays a big part in this. So let's rectify that. Let's spend some time together—with and without Timmy. That way you can see I want only what's best for him."

"You *have* been spending some time with him."

"I've been dabbling at it. I was trying to ease in, but that hasn't worked, so maybe a plunge is what we need."

"I go back to work part-time soon," she said. "Barb will be taking care of him in the mornings."

Even without the telepathy he sometimes wished for when dealing with Shaye, he knew she wasn't ready yet for him to take Timmy and care for him steadily. "Fine. Until you go back to work, we'll spend time together. When Barb begins babysitting, we can pick him up there and take him back to your place. Then we can talk about his day, maybe get some dinner together. It would be a start."

After she thought about his suggestion for a few moments, she agreed. "We could start there. There's something I have to ask you, though."

"What?"

"I know Julia wanted to have Timmy christened. I postponed it because of his health and the upside-down nature of everything. But now I'd like to do it. How do you feel about that?"

Although Julia had gone to church almost every Sunday, Dylan hadn't. Ever since their parents had been killed, his faith had been tested. He believed in what he could see, touch and feel.

However, he would do anything for Julia, even now. "We'd have to choose godparents."

"I thought about that. Do you have anyone in mind?"

"I think Walter would be honored to be godfather."

"I'd like to ask Gwen to be godmother."

"That works for me," Dylan said with a shrug. "How soon do you want to do it?"

"I can probably make an appointment with the minister tomorrow. Do you want to come along?"

Actually, he really didn't. But if parenthood was going to be about doing things he'd never done before, or didn't like to do, he might as well get used to it. "Sure, I'll come along. Just let me know what time."

Without another moment of thought, Shaye slid out of the desk and stood. When she picked up her denim jacket, Dylan took it from her and held it.

She slid into one sleeve and then the other. Reluctantly, he resisted the urge to touch her and move her hair away from her neck and kiss her nape.

As she faced him and they stood very close, he knew she was as aware of him as he was of her.

Suddenly her eyes met his. "I don't like what you're doing, Dylan, but I respect it."

Then she left the classroom and he heard the sound of her heels clicking as she walked down the hall. If he gained custody of Timmy, would he lose whatever bond he had with Shaye?

Chapter Eight

Last night Dylan had tossed and turned, thinking about his conversation—or confrontation—with Shaye the day before yesterday. He wanted custody of Timmy. The sad thing was, he also wanted Shaye in Timmy's life as his mother.

How could he have both?

If she could become reconciled to the idea of joint custody, she wouldn't be the only parent in Timmy's life.

They'd seen the minister yesterday and the christening was set for Sunday afternoon. Today he had plans to get his place ready for Timmy.

After he showered and dressed, Dylan looked around his apartment, trying to see it through a social worker's eyes. It was adequate, but it needed more. He had to have plenty of space for Timmy. Throughout the morning, he shifted, sorted and moved things around. Two file cabinets ended up in the living room. Somehow he fit the others, as well as his photographic equipment, into the computer room. Space was tight there, but it would have to do.

Finished with rearranging, he went shopping to buy a crib, changing table and bathtub like the one Shaye had used. All the while he considered what Julia and Will might have picked out. His heart ached as he chose the necessities, wishing he could converse one last time with Julia to understand her thoughts on raising a son. Finally, he realized all the wishing in the world wouldn't bring back his sister.

His last purchase was a four-foot kangaroo he thought any kid would love. Decorating definitely wasn't his forte. Along with the pictures for the show, he'd have some photographs framed of lions and elephants to hang on the walls.

Throughout the afternoon, he put the changing table and unassembled crib together. When he stuffed the mattress into the fitted sheet and settled it into the new crib, he looked at the baby's room with satisfaction.

He'd just hung up his phone after a conversation with Walter when his doorbell rang. Figuring maybe Lily had stopped by to discuss his show, he went to the door and opened it.

Shaye stood there, looking not at all comfortable, carrying a large shirt box.

"Hi! This is a surprise," he said.

"Are you busy?" she asked, looking ready to turn around and run.

"Not right now. Come on in."

When Shaye passed by him, he caught that scent of rose musk, so like the scent that came from the red rosebush in the yard. She was wearing a pretty sweater and slacks set in pink. With her hair pulled back and clasped with a wooden barrette, he realized it was getting longer. He liked it that way. As he remembered running his fingers through it, his gut clenched. They were alone here, and that was dangerous.

Playing host, he asked, "Can I get you something to drink?"

"No, I'm fine." She was looking around, taking in everything about his apartment, and he wondered why she was really here.

"I made some changes today. I turned my storage room into a nursery. This setup will work okay for now while Timmy's small, but I definitely need to look at some real estate. We'll need more room."

As he sent her clear signals now that he wasn't going to change his mind about custody, she paled a bit.

"See if you approve," he added casually, and motioned toward the new nursery.

Putting the box she'd brought on the sofa, she followed him. After she peeked inside the nursery, she mused quietly, "This looks ready for a baby."

"I have a bit more sprucing up to do. At least now Timmy can come over and I have a bed for him and anything else he might need. I'd like the name of the brand of formula you're using so I can stock up on that."

When she nodded and quickly turned away, he caught her arm. "Shaye, I know what this is doing to you. But give us a chance to work together for Timmy's sake."

Her eyes had filled with tears and he couldn't help but pull her close and hold her. At first she tried to push away, but he held on, finally feeling her relax against him. Moments later, with his hand on the back of her head, he tipped her face up to his.

"Don't," she protested softly, but she didn't push away.

He gave her a wry smile. "Don't kiss you? Don't make love to you? Don't push you out of Timmy's life?"

"All of the above," she murmured.

Hugging her again, he rested his jaw on top of her head. His heart was practically pounding out of his chest and he suspected hers might be, too. If he pushed the chemistry between them, if he took advantage of her when she was vulnerable, she'd never forgive him.

As he leaned away, he dropped his arms. "Come on. Show me what you brought."

Noticing that Shaye looked a little more relaxed when she sat on the sofa with the box on her lap, he realized with *her,* everything had to be out in the open. There were no games, no manipulation on her part, no "guess what I'm feeling" vibes. He liked that about her. He liked a whole lot of things about her.

Ignoring the fact that his bedroom wasn't that far away, he sat beside her on the sofa. "I just spoke with Walter and he said he'd love to be godfather to Timmy. He's free on Sunday."

"Do you have a list of the people you'd like to invite?"

When Dylan thought about it, he shook his head. "No. Walter's the only one."

"How about Lily?"

"I hadn't thought about asking her. Yes, she might like to come."

"How close are you?" Shaye asked.

She'd questioned him about Lily before and now he could see these questions weren't casual ones. That day they'd had lunch at the Silver Dollar, she apparently hadn't finished finding out what she wanted to know.

"We have a friendly business association."

When Shaye frowned, he knew the answer hadn't given her much information. "Ask me what you really want to know." For some reason, he had to make her put it into words.

Color came into her cheeks. "I thought maybe you had an ongoing relationship with her."

"That I slept with her when I returned to Wild Horse Junction?"

"Yes."

"No, I don't sleep with her when I come to town. You'd be surprised to learn my life is more celibate than you think. I told you before—I'm choosy and I'm careful."

"*We* weren't careful."

He ran his hand up and down the back of his neck. "No, we weren't. You just have to believe me when I say that never happened before, not like that."

Since she looked doubtful, he joked, "Do you want a list of the women I've slept with in the past five years?"

"No, of course not!"

"It's a short list. I have no reason to lie to you, Shaye, and I think by now, you'd realize I'm a straight-forward guy."

After she seemed to think about that, she said with a small sigh, "Yes, you are."

Although he was trying mightily hard not to kiss her, he couldn't resist running his hand down her cheek. "Lily and I have never been intimate."

As she ducked her head, Shaye moved away from his hand. Dropping the subject, she opened the lid of the box on her lap. "I wanted to show you what I bought for Timmy for the christening."

The little white suit she held up made Dylan smile. "He's going to look spiffy."

"I'll show you spiffy." She grinned and took a small white hat with a little brim from beneath more tissue paper.

Dylan laughed out loud. "And you think he's going to keep that on?"

"For about two seconds, but it will make a great picture if we can snap one."

"I just happen to have a few cameras—"

Now she laughed, too, and the awkwardness between them seemed to dissipate entirely. The attraction was still there, though, the chemistry pulsing between them. Yet there was camaraderie now and he found himself pleased they'd established that.

After putting down the hat, she lifted out little white shoes and socks from the box.

Dylan took them into his hand. They were so very

small. "It's hard to believe someday he'll be a strapping teenager with size eleven feet."

"Is that the size you wear?" she asked.

"You bet."

As they let the image of Timmy as a teenager settle in, he asked, "Did you invite Gwen to be godmother?"

"Yes, she was thrilled. I hope you don't mind, but I asked Kylie, too."

"Two godmothers?"

"I couldn't choose one over the other. Kylie has her plate full right now and I thought she might not want any part of it, but I brought it up and she said she'd love to be godmother, too. If need be, she and Gwen can take on the world."

"And Walter can whip it into shape. We'll have three fine people watching over Timmy."

"Yes, we will."

For a moment Dylan realized he liked thinking in terms of "we" with Shaye, but then he brushed the thought aside. "Are we going to have a reception after the christening? I can have it catered."

"Barb offered to let everyone come to her place. The church has a social hall, too."

"Why don't we have it in the social hall and I'll call a caterer. I'll feel as if I'm doing my part that way." He also wanted to make a statement. Shaye's family was large and enveloping and he didn't want them to swallow Timmy up. He intended to make a place for himself, starting now.

"The social hall it is," Shaye agreed, and he wondered if she'd finally learned he didn't give up easily and he always fought for what he wanted.

If she didn't know that about him yet, she soon would.

The church, which had been built in the late eighteen hundreds, held a quiet atmosphere of holiness and history. The antique pews shone with a time-honored patina. The floor was worn with the footsteps of church-goers. As Shaye held Timmy at the altar after the christening, Dylan snapped a few pictures, recording all of it. Then he zoomed in on Shaye's face, her Madonna smile, and snapped one of that, too.

"Intending to make copies of those?" Randall asked him as everyone else gathered around Timmy, including Walter. Lily had already made plans for the day and couldn't accept his invitation.

"I can." Earlier Shaye had introduced him to John. Now the younger brother, too, approached him unsmilingly. At six feet, he was broad-shouldered and fit.

In a low voice he asked, "Just what are you planning to do about Timmy? You're putting Shaye through hell."

Randall clasped his younger brother's arm. "Not here."

"Then where?" John asked. "It's not as if Malloy and I run into each other very often."

"It's fine," Dylan said. "Unless you're going to cause a scene that will upset everyone."

"Everyone's already upset. We've welcomed Timmy into our lives and now you want to claim him."

"Claim isn't the right word," Dylan replied. "I respect my sister's wishes in making Shaye his legal guardian. But she was my sister and he's my nephew. I'm going to be his dad. I won't cut Shaye or her family out of Timmy's life, but I will take responsibility for him."

"You can't take care of him like a mother could," John pointed out.

"No, I'll take care of him as a father would."

"That sounds great in theory, but we grew up without our mom and we know what it's like."

"I lost both of my parents. Don't you think I understand what life will be like for Timmy if he doesn't have a secure home?"

"You don't get it," John said angrily. "We had our father, but he worked all the time. Are you telling me you're going to quit running around the world and stay here? Exactly what are you going to do?"

"I don't have all the answers yet. Should Shaye and I share joint custody, I could still take assignments away from here."

"In other words, you're going to use her as a babysitter."

"What has you so ticked off?" Dylan asked, hoping to clear the air.

"*You* do. She's been in a tizzy ever since she met you."

"Watch it," Randall murmured to his brother.

With a slight flush, John went on anyway. "Something's going on between you two besides Timmy. You're sure trying to hide that, but we can all see it."

"You've had a family meeting about this?" Dylan asked with some consternation.

"Not exactly. Dad's oblivious, as always."

With that comment, Dylan glanced at Shaye's father who was talking to Walter now. Carson Bartholomew was a tall, thin man with gray hair and wire-rimmed spectacles. He looked like a doctor even without the lab coat. He seemed to be talking to everyone except Shaye. Dylan had felt awkwardness between father and daughter when she'd introduced him to the man.

Turning his full attention on John again, he warned him, "You and your brother can talk all you want, but whatever decisions Shaye and I have to make, whatever goes on between us, is between *us*."

"She's my sister and I'm going to watch out for her."

"I respect that. I know about sisters and wanting to protect them."

As if that fact was something John had forgotten, he replied less defensively, "Yes, I guess you do."

After John stepped away and joined the rest of his family once more, Randall apologized for him. "Sorry about that. He can be a hothead."

"I'd rather have him tell me what he's thinking instead of letting his resentment simmer."

Now Randall lowered his voice. "Shaye hasn't been involved with anyone since a guy when she was in grad school. She's probably not like most women you've met."

That was certainly true. If she hadn't been involved with a man since her grad school years, their encounter before he returned to Africa had been out of the ordinary for her. Why had she let it happen? Why had *he* let it happen?

Because at that moment they'd needed to reaffirm life? Because they'd been through a crisis and had to let off a little steam?

If only it were that simple.

Dylan decided to stow his camera in the car for the remainder of the afternoon. He wanted to be a participant in the celebration rather than an observer. Photographing wildlife, he felt as if he were part of the scene. Photographing humans was different—he had to be detached and set apart.

At his SUV, he thought about holding Timmy before the christening. He thought about taking off the little boy's white cap and retying one of his shoes. All day he'd been pushing thoughts of Julia away. Now sadness gripped him that she wasn't here to witness this first milestone moment in her child's life.

A few minutes later he entered the social hall. Conversation seemed to fill the room as guests moved through the buffet line. It was very obvious that Shaye's family had closed ranks around her. Randall and John were sitting on either side of her; Barb sat across from her. Walter had taken a seat at a second table next to Carson, who sat apart from his family. Other friends of the Bartholomews were here, too. Shaye had introduced Dylan to most of them but he didn't know any of them.

As Dylan moved to the buffet table, a soft but sweet voice at his elbow suddenly asked, "This is a difficult day for you, isn't it?"

Dylan looked at Kylie Warner. When he'd met her the first time, she'd been wearing jeans and a plaid blouse, and he'd thought she was pretty. Today, however, in a peasant-style gauzy dress, she was downright beautiful. The thing was, he noticed that with some detachment. His blood didn't race as it did when he looked at Shaye.

"Timmy was christened today," he said. "I'm happy about that."

"Christened with your father's name?"

"How did you know that?"

"Shaye told me. I knew Julia, too. Not well. Not like Shaye. I imagine you're thinking about *her* today, too."

There was a compassion in Kylie's eyes that was very different from the suspicion he saw in Gwen's and the wariness in Shaye's.

"I have been thinking about her...*and* Will."

Selecting vegetables from a tray and dip to go with them, Kylie noted, "You didn't ask very many guests to come."

"I don't have many connections in Wild Horse Junction. I've been away too much and too long. I called Will's mom to see if she could fly in, but she said the trip would be too difficult for her. I'm going to send her pictures."

When Kylie glanced over at the table where Shaye was sitting, she grimaced. "What are you going to do about *that?*"

Kylie's perception made him give her a wry smile. "I've been considering my options. I can take a chair over there and push my way in. I could put Shaye on the spot and invite her to sit at a table with me. I could appear at her elbow and tell her I'm going to take Timmy for a while. I could do nothing and let them all think I'm going to back off simply because they out-number me."

"What *are* you going to do?" Kylie asked again.

"That's a loaded question. I'm *not* going to kidnap

Timmy and run off to Tibet with him and raise him on a mountaintop. I think that's what all of them are afraid of."

"Wouldn't you be afraid if you were in Shaye's shoes?"

"I know she's afraid," Dylan conceded. "But in the long run, I can make life easier rather than harder for her. Timmy needs a mother's loving hand but he also needs a father's guidance and a male role model. If Shaye would just relax a little, I think she could see that."

"I don't think you understand just how much Shaye wanted to be a mother. While you were away, she'd begun planning her life with Timmy. Sharing him hadn't figured into any of her plans."

Dylan forgot the food on the table and faced Kylie. "I wouldn't be doing this if I didn't think it was the right thing to do. After I saw Timmy, after I absorbed what had happened to Julia, after I went back to a life I used to find fascinating but don't anymore, I realized I couldn't walk away from Timmy. I don't want to walk away."

After a pensive moment, Kylie said sincerely, "I think Timmy's lucky to have you in his life."

"I wish Shaye felt that way."

"She needs time to come to grips with you being here. Eventually she'll realize that if Timmy has two people who want to love and protect him, that has to be better than just having one person."

When Dylan saw the understanding in Kylie's eyes, he knew she was speaking from personal experience, but he didn't know her well enough to ask about it.

Suddenly their attention was drawn to Shaye's table where Timmy was fussing. Several small cries soon became a howl.

"That's what I need," Dylan said with a grin. "An opening. It was good talking to you."

"You, too. I figured if you're going to be in and out of Shaye's life, I should get to know you."

With Kylie's remark, he realized he wanted to be more "in" Shaye's life than out of it.

After he set his plate on a table near Walter, he went over to Shaye. "I'll walk him for a while so you can finish eating."

Instead of agreeing with him, she handed Timmy to him and then stood. "I think he needs to be changed."

"I can do that."

"There's a changing table in the ladies' room. I don't know if the men's room is equipped."

Dylan couldn't help but frown. "I think the world's set up for mothers and babies. Fathers aren't supposed to enter into the picture until it's time to sign up for Little League."

"That's the way lots of dads want it." She cut a glance toward her own.

After jiggling Timmy a little, Dylan lifted him to his shoulder and patted his back. The baby quieted. "Your dad's not acting like a doting grandfather."

Shaye's shoulders tensed a bit and her chin lifted. "My dad wasn't a doting *father*. Besides, I don't think he considers himself a grandfather."

"Because Timmy's not your biological child?"

"He'd never admit that, but yes, I think that's true. On the other hand, whether he's a grandfather or not wouldn't make any difference to his life. He's a doctor first and nothing else comes close."

She suddenly blushed. "I shouldn't have said anything. Dad's always taken care of us the best he knew how. After Mom died, he was lost and not equipped to take care of a family."

"He could have learned."

"He had three kids to feed and clothe and educate. Sure, he loved his work, but I think he always saw his place as the provider."

"You have a lot of mixed feelings where he's concerned."

"I guess I do. If he ever retires, maybe we'll get a chance to talk about them."

Seeing that Shaye wanted to believe that, Dylan knew if Carson had been closed off to his kids for all these years, retirement wouldn't change his personality.

Since Timmy's quiet spell was over and he was fussing again, Shaye motioned to the baby carry-all by her chair. "I'd better get that diaper, then he'll want a bottle. Would you like to feed him?"

"So I can prove to your friends and relatives that I'm capable?" He couldn't help the edge that sharpened his voice.

Shaye leaned close to him so he could hear her. "They need reassurance that your interest in him isn't just a whim."

"I don't have anything to prove to anyone except Timmy. Go get the diaper and I'll feed him in the room down the hall…away from everybody's prying eyes."

A half hour later Shaye went to find Dylan. After she'd changed Timmy, she'd let Dylan take him down the hall and she hadn't followed. She'd made herself go back to her table and finish eating.

As she left the social hall, she wondered why she'd told Dylan what she had about her father. She usually kept her feelings about him under wraps. What was the point in reliving history? Nothing would be changed by it—not her sense of aloneness that had been with her since her mother had died, not her childish dream that someday her dad would wrap his arms around her and tell her how much he loved her...that he was proud of her. She'd learned long ago not to base her actions on what someone else did or didn't say or do.

When she saw the open door to one of the meeting rooms, she stopped and approached it more slowly. At the doorway, she saw Dylan sitting in an old wooden captain's chair, Timmy in the crook of his arm. The empty bottle sat on the floor. Dylan was so big and Timmy was so small. She couldn't help studying Dylan's features, his thick hair, his very broad shoulders in his suit jacket. Could a man care for a baby as well as a woman? Did it have to be a competition?

Dylan looked up and caught her watching him. Their eyes collided.

She shook down to her white pumps.

Recovering from the impact as best she could, she asked, "How's he doing?"

"He finished the bottle. He must have been hungry."

As she came into the room, Dylan transferred Timmy to his shoulder to burp him. The burp came almost immediately.

"Good boy," they both said at the same time.

When Dylan laughed, she smiled and she wished she could separate the bond over Timmy from the bond between the two of them. Was there even a bond between the two of them? They'd made love once. She'd never forget what had happened that day. But she suspected Dylan could live in the moment much more easily than she could...and move on to the next.

As he stood, she automatically reached out for Timmy.

"Your arms feel empty without him?" Dylan asked.

She nodded.

"I had a short talk with Kylie. I got the impression she's not taking sides. Does that bother you?"

"Do you mean, do I think she's being disloyal? No, she's being Kylie. She probably has more sense than Gwen and I put together."

"Even though she's not happy herself?"

"I think that's going to change."

"And that's all you're going to say," Dylan said with a smile.

Carefully taking Timmy from his shoulder, Dylan gave him to Shaye. In the transfer, his hand brushed her breast. He was close enough for her to smell his male scent mixed with aftershave. In his charcoal suit today, he looked distinguished and handsome.

"I've been thinking," he said when the transfer was completed. "The good weather is supposed to hold through tomorrow. The temperature is supposed to be in the seventies. How would you like to take a ride and hike with me? Timmy, too. I can buy one of those carriers that I've seen walkers use."

"Hiking with a baby? Where do you have in mind?"

"Along Mustang Creek. Babies need fresh air and sunshine, and Timmy needs a spirit of adventure. We should start him early."

A spirit of adventure. Maybe she needed to find hers.

She wondered if Dylan realized they'd have to take along all of Timmy's supplies and that this adventure might be a little different from what he was used to. But there was no point warning him. She'd just let him experience it.

Chapter Nine

The next day, the expression on Dylan's face was priceless as he motioned to the paraphernalia Shaye had collected to take on their hike. "All that has to go?"

She couldn't help grinning. "Babies need a lot of supplies."

"What a bunch of bull." He was already scanning the diaper carry-all bag and the grocery bag filled with odds and ends she might need.

"I'm going to consolidate everything into a backpack. One of us can carry Timmy and the other will have to carry the backpack."

She couldn't help but notice how rugged Dylan looked today. She'd be spending hours with him. Her tummy somersaulted. "How long will we be gone?"

"About three hours. A mile in and a mile out. Any problem with that?"

Dressing Timmy in his sweater, she answered, "No problem. But what if Timmy cries and we can't get him settled?"

"He'll keep the bears away."

Her head jerked up and she met Dylan's gaze. He obviously couldn't help but laugh at her expression. "Relax, Shaye. We'll be fine. If we make enough noise, animals usually head in the other direction."

"Usually?" She drawled the word.

He grinned. "Most of the time. Now, come on. I have picnic supplies in the cooler. When we reach the trail area, I'll have to pack those in the backpack, too."

As she attached Timmy's little hat, she shook her head. "Are you sure this is worth the trouble?"

Crossing to her, Dylan capped her shoulder with his large, warm hand. "Trust me."

That was the whole crux of the matter. She didn't know if she could. She trusted her brothers to have her well-being at heart. She trusted Gwen and Kylie and colleagues she worked with, but when it came down to bachelors and men she might date, when it came down to Dylan in particular, trust was a foreign concept.

Twenty minutes later, after they'd parked in a gravel lot that serviced more than one hiking trail, Shaye marveled at how much Dylan had fit into his backpack.

Hefting it in one hand, he decided, "Timmy's lighter, but I'm probably more sure on my feet as we're hiking. It's up to you to decide what you want to carry."

On this, she did trust Dylan to keep Timmy safe. He

was used to hiking, she wasn't. "I can handle the pack. We're not going that far."

Dylan nodded as if that was the conclusion he'd come to.

The trail was wide enough that they could walk side by side. At once, Shaye could tell Dylan was in his element. He was sure-footed as his gaze examined the scene, as if he'd experienced it many times before and was looking for something new.

She tried to see the area through his eyes. After scanning the west beyond the lodge-pole pines and the Douglas firs, her gaze shifted to the east. Green leaves of gambel oaks waved in the breeze. Those trees could handle almost anything Wyoming dished out—including wind and drought. Alone, could she handle everything parenthood dished out? Did she want to cut Dylan out of Timmy's life?

She had to admit she didn't.

Sun lined the path as they walked and brushed by choke cherries with new growth turning red. Buttercups and goldenrod dotted grassy areas, and Shaye realized she'd stopped worrying and was simply enjoying being outdoors.

Suddenly, Dylan pulled a small camera from his pocket and snapped a picture of her.

"What are you doing?"

"How long has it been since you went hiking?"

Shrugging, she hated to admit the truth. "A few years."

"Then we need a record of this. You'll want to tell Timmy about the first time you brought him here."

When she rolled her eyes, Dylan took her elbow,

stopping her. "A child's history is more important to him than you can ever imagine. In the shuffle of what happened to my parents and the foster homes, Julia and I lost all of our family photographs. I want Timmy to see the world through his eyes and ours. I want him to be able to see the world close up, far away and from every perspective."

As always, she was fascinated by Dylan and wished she wasn't. His hand on her arm heated up her entire being and she had to admit he had a point.

Taking the camera from his hand and moving a few steps away so she could think more clearly, she replied, "Then it's only fair I snap a few pictures of you, too."

His grin was crooked. "Uh, oh. What have I started?"

She brought the camera to her eye. "Turn a bit sideways so I can include Timmy, too."

After that, their hike took a little longer than expected because they stopped frequently to take pictures of the canyons rising to the cerulean sky, a deer nibbling at brush, Timmy dozing in the carrier. Shaye felt as if Dylan were showing her a world she'd never seen, not just scenery but a different way of looking at everything that was around her.

Why had she been so afraid to come today? Not because an unpredictable moose might charge them, not because the temperature would be too cold or too hot for Timmy. Rather, she'd been afraid her feelings for Dylan would grow even deeper, complicating her life and Timmy's, complicating the issue of custody that had to be settled. Most of all, she'd been afraid today would shatter the remains of the wall she'd built around her heart so she wouldn't get hurt again. Dylan had been battering that wall ever since she'd met him.

They heard Mustang Creek before they saw it and Timmy seemed to hear it, too, because he looked around. She tried to introduce him to new shapes and colors every day—his vision was maturing and he seemed delighted by everything they passed on the trail.

"Lots of special things to see, aren't there?" she asked him, and he cooed back as if he understood her.

"I bought a baby book," Dylan remarked.

"What did you want to know?"

"What happens when. You know—what he's supposed to be doing at four months, five months, a year, two."

"Every baby advances at his own speed."

"I know, but I didn't only want to know what he should be doing, I wanted to know what *I* should be doing—like rattling keys at him, calling him by name, watching whether he notices the sound of my voice."

"You not only bought the book, you read it. I'm impressed."

When Dylan glanced at her, he could see she was teasing him. "Good. I like impressing pretty girls."

She couldn't keep a blush from coming to her cheeks. "I'm not pretty. I'm ordinary."

He stopped short. "Who ever told you that?"

"Nobody ever told me, exactly. It's a feeling I got. You know, being around my brothers' friends."

"If they didn't hit on you, they were afraid to because of your brothers. There are bonds of brotherhood you don't step over."

She'd never thought about it that way. "I never dated much. I didn't even go to my prom."

"I'm telling you, Shaye, you had two brothers to watch over you. That's intimidating to anybody who'd want to take you out."

After the christening, she'd seen her brothers talking with Dylan. "Do they intimidate *you?*"

"No."

As her gaze met Dylan's, they laughed, and Dylan had to admit, "John's not as subtle as Randall."

"What did he say to you?"

"Nothing that would help family relations. Tell me something. Did your dad ever tell you you were pretty?"

Her mind swerved from her brothers to her father and all the joking was over. "No, he didn't."

"There you go," Dylan said. "That's why you think you're not pretty."

"I think that's a little too simplistic."

"I don't. I think you became an independent, caring woman because of your brothers and in spite of your dad."

"Have you given this a lot of thought?" How much did he think about her? He was in and out of her mind twenty-four hours a day and had been ever since February.

"Some," he admitted, looking at her and not turning away.

Breaking eye contact, she stared ahead. There was something about looking into Dylan's eyes that simply made the world higher, brighter, wider and bigger. The feeling terrified her.

They'd soon covered the mile, and Timmy still seemed content. Maybe he *did* need fresh air and new sights. Maybe he needed more than she could give him.

When Dylan seemed to be headed for one particular spot, she soon saw why. Cottonwoods and river birches grew along the creek bed. Mustang Creek began in the canyons of the Painted Peaks and wound down, at some spots wide, here much narrower. The day had turned practically balmy and only a light breeze stirred her hair. She'd tied it back so it wouldn't get in the way. Dressed in her jeans and cotton shirt, a practical sweater tied around her waist, she wondered how Dylan looked at her. As a desirable woman? Or as a woman who wanted to be Timmy's mom?

They stopped and Dylan suggested, "I thought we could set up lunch here."

She couldn't have picked a better spot. She couldn't have chosen a more beautiful day. As they spread out a thin blanket Dylan pulled from his backpack, she asked, "Are you always this prepared?"

"I have to be prepared when I go on a shoot, otherwise the whole trip could be wasted. In this case, I just want you to relax and see that Timmy doesn't have to be kept inside and protected too much."

"In other words, you had an ulterior motive."

"I had an objective. How am I doing?"

She took Timmy's bottle in its own insulated cooler from the backpack as well as the sandwiches and the bottles of water. "You're doing great. This is a lovely break. But I still have to wonder how comfortable we'll be if we walk back and he's fussing all the way."

"Let's take him out of that carrier and give him playtime on the blanket before we eat. He'll sleep on the trek out."

Almost immediately, she figured out what Dylan was up to because she often did the same thing at home. With Timmy on his stomach, Dylan pulled a rattle from the backpack and shook it. Timmy raised his head. Pushing up on his arms, he arched his back a bit and kicked his legs.

"Soon, he'll be doing push-ups," Dylan said with a smile.

"I'm waiting for him to roll over on his own," Shaye added.

As Dylan shook the rattle again, Timmy gurgled at him.

Dylan asked nonchalantly, "What are you going to do about working?"

In spite of her intentions to keep the conversation casual, Shaye knew her back straightened as her defenses came up. "I have money saved. I can work part-time for a few months, but then I'll have to go back full-time."

"With child support, you could permanently work part-time."

"With child support, I'd feel as if I owe you."

She could feel Dylan's gaze on her. "What's more important, your pride or being with Timmy more hours in the day?"

At this precise moment, her pride and being with Timmy was a toss-up. She knew it shouldn't be, but she didn't want to depend on Dylan. She'd depended on Chad. She'd started making him her world and he'd left for India without her. After her mother died, she'd wanted to depend on her father and had looked to him for comfort and a safe haven. But she'd found neither. And her brothers? In a way, *they'd* always depended on *her.* At first, for someone to replace their mom and then later she'd felt the burden of simply keeping her family together, not letting them all go off in different directions and forget about each other.

"What?" Dylan asked gently, turning Timmy onto his back, then coming to sit by her side.

"Nothing," she murmured.

"Don't lie to me, Shaye. Your thoughts are clicking through your brain so fast, your eyes are changing color."

"My eyes are brown."

"Your eyes sometimes have golden sparks. They're amber, not simply brown."

"Dylan…" His name was a protest, but a weak one.

His arm went around her shoulders. "Tell me you don't want me to kiss you."

Looking at him like this, studying the lines around his eyes, his hair tousled from the wind, the scent of him seeping into her with each breath, she couldn't tell him that. She was beginning to believe Dylan and run-of-the-mill kisses didn't go together. If he'd just crush his lips against hers, quickly push his tongue into her mouth and then back away, she'd be fine. But he never did that.

So close to her now she could feel his breath, Dylan stroked her cheek. The spot tingled and in spite of herself she wondered what came next. His lips were hot and when they lingered at the corner of her mouth, she stayed perfectly still. Slowly his tongue came out and whispered across her upper lip, then lingered on her lower one. Eventually he slid it between the two as if he were giving *her* the power to bar his entrance or welcome him. She knew *he* had all the power, and that almost made her pull away. But just then, the tip of his tongue slid across the seam of her lips and she moaned at the exquisite sensation of it. Opening to him, she finally knew she was falling in love with Dylan, and it was a tumble she didn't want to take. Yet as his tongue stroked against hers, she couldn't resist the power of the chemistry between them and her arms went around his neck.

As Dylan's tongue stroked hers, the sounds of the creek seemed to become louder. The rustle of leaves swept away every other thought in her head. Timmy's happy gurgles let her fall into Dylan with a suddenness that surprised even her. Captivated by every sensual texture of his lips and tongue and arms, she wanted to be here with him and nowhere else.

Dylan didn't stop with simply pushing his tongue against hers. He stroked and dipped into nooks and crannies, making her ache, urging her to long for so much more than a kiss. When his hand slipped from her shoulder, swept over her collar and rested on her neckline, she knew he wanted to become more intimate.

All she had to do was pull away. All she had to do was say no. All she had to do was relegate Dylan to a part of her life that was separate from her feelings and wishes and longings and dreams.

She was powerless to do that.

Dylan trailed his hand down her blouse slowly as if

he enjoyed simply the act of it rather than hurrying toward what came next. Would he do the same if he made love to her again? Instead of fast and frenzied, would they be able to go slow?

Her anticipation grew. Kissing Dylan became an art that she participated in as fully as he did. When his fingers slid to her breast, when his palm rested on it, she felt overwhelmed with the sensual intake of all of it.

Suddenly, Timmy's rattle rattled. There was a small cry and Shaye shut down the intimacy she and Dylan were sharing.

Only Timmy should matter to her, now.

Wasn't Dylan using the oldest form of persuasion to pull her into his world? To make her see what he wanted her to see? If her perspective was so clouded by him, she'd do anything he wanted.

Pulling away, she went to Timmy without checking the expression on Dylan's face.

After she picked up the baby, she held him close, crooned to him and cut Dylan out of her world. The problem was, he knew it, and he wouldn't let her do it. She felt his body next to her...she felt his arm go around her. With Timmy in her arms, it was hard to shrug away.

"He's fine," Dylan murmured.

"I'm not," she whispered back.

"You can't keep denying how much we want each other."

"I can't deny that you're trying to persuade me to give you joint custody."

"What just happened here has *nothing* to do with

joint custody." He sounded angry and when she brought her gaze to his, she knew he was.

"You think I'm misjudging your intentions?" she asked. "Maybe you don't even know you *have* them."

"I'm not your father, Shaye. He used you to take care of your brothers when he didn't know what else to do. I'm not the guy who dropped you at the whiff of a good professional opportunity. Look past them and look at me."

"And see what, Dylan? You're going to settle down in Wild Horse Junction and give up your career to become domestic? I don't think so. So our relationship is convenient for you. You want fatherhood that's convenient for you. Heck, I don't even know if you want a relationship. Maybe all you want is another go at sex because you know I'm safe."

"Safe? You're anything *but* safe," he muttered.

"What do you mean? I haven't slept around."

"No, you haven't, and that's why you aren't safe. I know what you want, Shaye. You want what Julia wanted—a man who works nine to five, is home every night and weekends, who doesn't have a hobby beyond watching football on Sundays."

"I never said—"

"No, you didn't, but neither you nor Julia had the home you wanted when you were kids. You want to create it now and it's probably what you want to give Timmy."

"Of course it's what I want for Timmy! I want him to have security and stability, to feel protected and to know he belongs. That's what *every* child deserves."

Dylan shook his head sadly. "There are different ways to give a child all of that, other than the traditional, other than two parents, a picket fence and a swing in the backyard that's the most excitement a child can get."

"Maybe you don't want to recreate your childhood," she said. "Maybe you're still trying to escape from it. Maybe being an adventurer is nothing more than being a kid who never grew up."

The expression on Dylan's face told her she'd crossed a boundary. He wore a cold expression now that she'd never seen, and in the space of a second, she'd put so much distance between them that they were lifetimes apart.

Rising to his feet, he stood for a moment and looked out over the creek, up into the mountains.

Then he stooped to take Timmy from her. "I'm going to show him the water, let him feel some tree bark, talk to him about the sky and where it could take him. There are kids who dream about becoming astronauts. Of course, there are parents who squelch those dreams because becoming an astronaut might not be safe."

When Dylan strode away from her, her dreams and her world were in his hands.

Holding Timmy on her lap, playfully patting his hands together, Shaye sat in Gwen's bedroom that evening watching her pack a suitcase. "So, where are you going this time?"

"Jackson Hole. I'm speaking to physical education teachers."

"How long will you be gone?"

"Five days. I'm taking my vacation—two days for work, three days for me. I'm going to drive and sightsee."

"That could be a long trip alone."

"I'll be fine. I have my cell phone, though it probably won't work in a lot of the area. But my car's fairly new, the weather's good and I'll have everything I need stowed in the back." After stuffing a sweatshirt into her suitcase, she glanced at Shaye. "You're postponing the inevitable."

"Not inevitable." She shifted Timmy to her other knee, where she played with his toes and made him giggle.

"You didn't come over here to talk about my trip or my lack of company on it. What's up?"

"Am I so absolutely transparent? Dylan says I don't know how to lie."

Laughing, Gwen smoothed a pair of jeans into her luggage. "That's probably a good thing. Why would you want to?"

Shaye sighed. "I never thought about it before, but Dylan stirs up too many of my emotions. The problem is, especially around him, I can't even deny them. It's as if he can see whatever I'm feeling...or thinking."

"Is he still adamant about joint custody?"

"Yes. What concerns me now is the method he's using to get it."

"What method? Has he hired a cutthroat lawyer other than Walter?"

Fiddling with Timmy's playsuit, she replied, "No, I'm not talking about legal maneuvering."

Gwen closed the lid to her travel case and sat next to it on the bed. "Unload, Shaye. What's going on?"

After a brief hesitation she asked, "Have you ever been so attracted to a man you could forget your name?"

Gwen thought about it, then replied, "I had a pretty deep crush on Cal Winters when I was in eighth grade."

"Gwen, be serious! When you were engaged to Mark, did you think about anything but kissing him?"

"Uh, oh. You've got it bad."

"I don't need editorial comment. Answer my question."

"Kissing is just part of what we did, as well as…other things. Both of us were very reasonable about it. I mean, we both had busy lives. When we went on dates, kissing at the end of them was kind of expected." She suddenly stopped. "Maybe one of the reasons he didn't show up at the wedding was because we didn't have enough passion. But I always thought passion was overrated. Isn't compatibility more important?"

It had taken Gwen two years to heal and get her self-confidence back where men were concerned. She still wasn't dating now, so Shaye knew she wasn't entirely over what had happened.

"Were you compatible with Mark?"

"I thought so. With him being a physician's assistant, we had lots to talk about and understood what our jobs required of us. Our schedules were even similar."

"So why didn't it work? What did Mark tell you when you confronted him?"

"He said he got the feeling we both weren't fully invested in the idea of marriage. I didn't know what that meant, then. I figured he got cold feet and was commitment-phobic. But as time has passed, I think *I* was the problem," Gwen said softly, lowering her gaze to her lap, then bringing it back to Shaye's. "My background plays into it."

Gwen's biological parents had abandoned her, Shaye knew. They'd left her in a church and no one had ever seen them again. Then Gwen had been adopted by the Langworthys. When she was ten, her mother fell in love with another man and moved, eventually starting another family and forgetting about Gwen and her dad. Because of it, Gwen's father had turned to alcohol. Now he was sober, but his daughter didn't expect him to stay that way. He'd fallen off the wagon too many times. A couple of years ago she'd stopped enabling him, stopped taking care of him, had moved out of the family home into a house of her own. All of it had left its mark. Gwen was even more independent than Shaye, more assertive, more determined to make sure she didn't need anyone.

Now Shaye asked, "Did you push Mark away?"

After a considering moment, her friend replied, "Not intentionally. Maybe instead of pushing him away, I just couldn't open up enough. I don't know. I guess I'll *never* know."

"Do you think it's true that opposites attract? And when they do, there are more sparks than in an easier relationship?"

"Do you think you and Dylan have crack and sizzle because you're opposites? I think there's a lot more to it than that. I think great love affairs are few and far between, that most people don't know true passion or real desire. To answer your question, I never have."

After Gwen stood, she picked up Timmy and lifted

him high in the air. When he giggled, she smiled and brought him close to her, holding him in the crook of her arm. "So, you think Dylan is using your attraction to him to convince you to do what he wants?"

"I don't want to think that."

"Yes, I think you do," Gwen disagreed. "If you keep questioning his motives, you won't give in to him. If you have doubts about him, that makes it easier to push him away."

"What am I going to do?" It was a rhetorical question and Shaye didn't expect an answer, but Gwen gave her one.

"You're going to put Timmy first and guard your heart."

"I can easily put Timmy first, but when I'm around Dylan, guarding my heart seems to be a monumental endeavor."

Gwen went completely still. "Have you fallen in love with him?"

"I think I have," she admitted.

Still holding Timmy, Gwen put a hand on her shoulder. "I bought a half gallon of ice cream just for this occasion. Come on. Problems can always be solved over a good double fudge."

Chapter Ten

On Saturday, as Shaye stood in the outdoor booth selling baked goods for church, she saw Dylan striding toward her. In jeans and a dark brown shirt, he looked as good as he had all week when he'd come to her town house to spend time with Timmy. As he'd visited, she'd watched from afar, pretending to be busy. They hadn't *really* spoken to each other since their confrontation at Mustang Creek.

Now, here he was at Horse and Buggy Days, standing in front of her booth, unobtrusively appraising her white-eyelet peasant blouse and long red-and-blue gingham skirt.

"Hi," he said, as if they were meeting for the first time in a long while.

"Hi." Not knowing what else to say or do, she motioned to the packages of brownies in front of her. "Want to buy baked goods for a good cause?"

"What's the good cause?"

"All our donations will go for baskets for needy families over the holidays."

Pointing to a packet of two brownies, he took out his wallet. "I'll take that one."

She was about to slip it into a bag when he shook his head.

"I missed lunch, so I'll eat them now." After he handed her a few bills and told her to keep the change, she watched him unwrap the brownies.

Traffic had slowed and she didn't have anyone else to take her attention away from Dylan. As he ate, savoring the chocolate dessert, she couldn't take her gaze from his lips. Those lips could give *so* much pleasure.

"Have you had lunch yet?" he asked.

"No, I haven't. Someone's supposed to relieve me soon."

"I need the main course now that I've had dessert. Do you want to get something together?"

She hated the tension between them...as well as the wall. Maybe they could rediscover a friendlier footing. "That would be nice." She motioned to her outfit. "If you don't mind walking around with someone who escaped from another era."

"I don't mind." There was a warmer quality to his voice today that hadn't been there all week. "Maybe we should take one of the horse and buggy rides and get into the real flavor of the day."

The town had gone all-out. Besides the stands selling everything from pottery to chili, activities had been organized for the whole day. There had been a baseball game that morning and games for the children as well as a petting zoo and horse and buggy rides. Also, artisans in selected shops were holding demonstrations of crafts handed down from generation to generation such as candle-making, saddle-crafting, pottery-sculpting and jewelry design. Even the waitresses at the Silver Dollar were dressed in clothes that had come from the eighteen hundreds.

Finished with the brownies, Dylan asked, "Is Timmy at Barb's?"

Shaye nodded. "Randall's here somewhere with the kids. After I pick up Timmy, Barb's going to come into town for the evening celebration."

"The fiddling and the fireworks?"

"I think there's a country band, too."

"Were you planning to join them?"

"Actually, I wasn't."

"You were going to go home, give Timmy a bath and call it a night."

She became defensive. "Is there anything wrong with that?"

"No. I just don't understand why you hibernate."

"Maybe I prefer my own company. Maybe I just want to spend some quiet time with my..." She was about to say her son.

"With your son," Dylan finished. "Don't be afraid to say it, Shaye."

"I'm not afraid. Damn it, Dylan, you've ruined a perfectly good afternoon."

Swearing was foreign to her and now she couldn't believe he'd gotten her so frustrated she'd done it in front of him.

But instead of countering her frustration with his own, he smiled. "You're jumping to conclusions. I'm not going to ruin your afternoon. In fact, I'm going to make it better for both of us. Let's have a late lunch, take a horse and buggy ride and go get Timmy and bring him back here. Or do you really want to spend the evening alone...with him?" he tacked on, but she knew what he meant.

"That depends. Are we going to argue all day?"

"No, we're not going to argue."

"And I don't want Timmy scared at the fireworks tonight."

"Fine. We'll leave before the fireworks start. Music won't hurt him, will it?" The question had a tinge of sarcasm, then he immediately raised both hands. "Sorry. I promise I won't take swipes at the way you want to spend your time."

"Music will be fine, as long as it's not too loud."

He laughed and shook his head in exasperation.

Business suddenly picked up as a few passersby stopped for snacks or baked goods. As Dylan stood in the shade of the feed store's front overhang, he watched Shaye. She looked pretty in the feminine blouse and long skirt. This week had been tense, to say the least, and although he'd enjoyed the time he'd spent with Timmy, he'd been aware that Shaye hadn't been that far away. Her accusation that he'd used the chemistry between them to get what he wanted had cut deep…too deep. Perhaps because the accusation was partly true, he had to admit.

If he and Shaye were on the same wavelength, in and out of bed, wouldn't that make life easier for everybody?

Yet, the sonar he'd developed where Shaye was concerned, the deep twisting ache in his gut whenever he was around her, the arousal he couldn't deny, had never been part of any plan. It just *was*.

When the next volunteer showed up to relieve Shaye, all Dylan knew was that he wanted a tension-free afternoon with her.

Finished at the booth, she exited the back and came over to where he was standing. "Do you still want to get something to eat?"

"Do you think I changed my mind about being hungry, or about spending time with you?"

"Either. Both."

"Once I design a plan, I don't change my mind."

"Inflexible, are we?" she joked lightly.

"I don't know about you, but when I'm determined, I don't let much stand in my way."

"I'm finding that out." Her tone was wry, as if she didn't appreciate that quality about him.

He motioned to the next block and then across the street where more booths were located that were selling food.

"So, what's your pleasure? Chili, hot wings, corn dogs, burgers?"

"Did you ever try Mrs. Garcia's hot wings?" Shaye was looking across the street at a stand where a line waited to pay for their servings.

"I don't know if I have."

"Joanie Garcia caters small parties and family get-togethers. Her wings are so hot, you need a fire hydrant close by, turned on full-force."

"Hot wings are out?" he asked, his brows raised.

"No, I didn't say that. I like a good fire now and then, but—"

When Shaye stopped midsentence, Dylan turned his attention from the line at the hot wing stand, to her. "Shaye?"

Her eyes were wide, her lips slightly parted and she was staring across the street.

He recognized the man. It was her father and he had his arm around a younger, very pretty blonde.

"I don't believe it," Shaye murmured.

At that moment, Carson Bartholomew leaned close to the woman as if he were whispering in her ear. The couple laughed. Carson's arm curled around his date's waist, and he brought her close to him as they waited their turn in the queue at the stand.

Dylan wasn't going to pretend he hadn't seen what Shaye had seen. "Do you know her?"

"No, I don't know her. I wonder what he's doing with her!"

"They look as if they've known each other for a while."

"Longer than a first date."

"Do you want to go over there?"

"No! That's the last thing I want to do."

"Does your father dating bother you?"

"No, I'm just surprised, that's all. And she's very …young. My age."

He couldn't help but smile. "You can tell that from this distance?"

"My eyesight's twenty-twenty. I can tell by the way she moves."

Settling a hand on her shoulder, he nudged Shaye to face him. "Come on, let's get some lunch. There's a fried chicken stand in the other direction."

Finally nodding, Shaye responded softly, "That sounds like a good idea."

She was very quiet as Dylan bought two chicken dinners including biscuits, coleslaw and mashed potatoes. They headed toward picnic tables that had been set up under canopies on the town square. After they were seated, they ate and Dylan left Shaye to her thoughts.

As residents of Wild Horse Junction milled about, sat at the other tables and left again, Dylan finally asked Shaye, "Would you like something else to drink?"

She'd finished her lemonade and now looked at it as if she wondered where it had gone. "No, I'm fine."

But she wasn't. Every once in a while she glanced down the street and he wondered if she was hoping for a confrontation with her dad…or planning to avoid it.

About to suggest they go for that buggy ride, he gathered their plates. When he looked up, John Bartholomew saw them and waved.

He approached with a smile that faded when Shaye asked, "Did you know Dad is dating someone?"

With a grimace, Shaye's brother lowered himself onto the bench across from her. "Sure you want to talk about this now?" He glanced at Dylan.

"Yes, now is fine."

With a shrug, her brother answered, "Yeah, I knew. It's been going on about a month now."

"Why didn't you tell me?"

"Because I knew you'd be upset."

"I'm not upset."

Her brother's brows quirked up and he stared at her steadily.

Raising her hands in a resigned gesture, she protested, "I'm not upset. I just wish he'd told me. I'm surprised, that's all. He's always been too busy for a personal life."

As he fingered a straw wrapper that had been lying loose on the table, John suggested, "That could change. He's thinking about retiring."

"Oh, really? *That* doesn't happen over night. When did he decide that?"

"Around Christmas, he first mentioned it to me."

"Does Randall know all this?"

Instead of his usual blustery self, John looked a bit sheepish. "Yeah, I think he does. He definitely knows Dad's dating Nicole."

"Nicole who?"

"Nicole Taylor. She's a bigwig at the bank."

"How big a wig can she be when she's probably only thirty?"

Dylan could tell John was suppressing a grin. "She's thirty-five."

"She could be his daughter."

"Yeah, I guess so, and that's probably the lure. He wants to feel young again."

As if uncomfortable with what he'd told Shaye, or her reaction to it, John untangled his long legs from the bench and stood. "Randall and I decided we should stay out of it. You should probably do the same."

"Let's see. Our father is dating a woman who could become our stepmother and you think we should pretend we don't notice?"

"I didn't say we should pretend anything, but it's *his* life."

"You know what, John? I think all protective brothers should be walked to Wild Horse Canyon and left there for a while until they realize families should communicate."

Raising his hands as if to ward off Shaye's words, her brother half-teased, "That's it. I'm out of here." With a regretful look at Dylan that said *he* could deal with Shaye, John ambled down the street.

Beside Shaye, his shoulder against hers, Dylan could feel her pent-up frustration.

She blew out a breath. "John keeping silent doesn't surprise me, but Randall doesn't usually keep me in the dark."

"You're assuming they kept you in the dark on purpose."

"Of course, they did it on purpose. They probably made a pact. They did that when they were kids. John would get a bad grade and he'd swear Randall to secrecy. Randall would buy a new stereo system with money he was supposed to be saving for college and John would help him hook it up in his closet. John would miss his curfew and Randall would tell me he was already in bed. I always caught on," she added.

"They knew you'd find out about this, too."

"Yeah, later, rather than sooner. Don't they realize I've always felt as if they've excluded me from their club? Doesn't Dad realize I've always cared about him, but he's never acted as if he cared about me?" Immediately she looked sorry she'd said it. "Did *that* ever sound whiney." She gave a fake laugh and got to her feet. "I learned a long time ago that Dad keeps his life separate from ours."

"Has your dad ever said 'thank you'?" Dylan asked. She blinked. "For what?"

"For you raising your brothers without his help."

All of Shaye's indignation and frustration vanished in a moment and her eyes filled with tears. When she shook her head, Dylan wrapped his arm around her shoulders, wondering how much of Shaye's upset was due to her dad dating a younger woman and her brothers cutting her out of the information loop. Or, rather, was it due to everything that had happened in the past five months? Something told him she needed a break before she went back to work. He'd been mulling over an idea for himself but maybe he needed to include Shaye.

Turning her toward him, he asked, "How would you like to take a break from the real world?"

"Wouldn't that be lovely," she quipped.

"I mean it. I was going camping for a couple of days. If you go along, it could just be overnight—a night without any responsibilities. I want to photograph the mustangs in the Big Horns. We could leave in the afternoon and be back the following afternoon. Twenty-four hours away from everything that makes you crazy and stressed."

"I can't leave Timmy," she protested.

"I know you love taking care of him. But don't you think you could use a few hours of downtime just for yourself? Once you go back to work, you'll feel guilty you're not with Timmy twenty-four hours a day and you'll put even more energy into giving him what he needs. That energy has to come from somewhere. You can't drain yourself dry, Shaye, and I think that's what you've been doing."

Some part of her must have known he was right because she wasn't giving him an out-and-out no. "How do you know where to find the horses?"

"I know their watering holes. I know where they feed. Believe me, I can find them."

"I'll have to ask Barb if she can take care of Timmy. Maybe I could keep my niece and nephew overnight to repay her."

"We could take them to the rodeo in Cody some night."

After she gave it a little more thought, she asked, "You think I'm rough and tough enough for a camping and hiking trip? What about the sleeping arrangements?"

"We'll just figure it out as we go."

Shaye seemed to accept that. "All right. I'll talk to Barb when we get back. When do you want to go?"

"Tomorrow."

"Seize the moment?" she asked, a bit uneasily.

"The weather's supposed to be good tomorrow. We should take advantage of it."

His pragmatism seemed easier for her to accept than the idea that she should be a free spirit and go where life led her. "You're afraid I'll change my mind?"

"No, I'm afraid you'll make a list of the pros and cons, and in the pro column you'll forget to add the mountains and the canyons and the color of the horses' manes, the air and the exercise, the stars and the sense of freedom."

Laughing, she protested, "Stop! Let's take that buggy ride before I'm overwhelmed by the pros."

Suddenly he was struck by the longing to show Shaye every advantage of living with the spirit of adventure. He wasn't even going to try to guess what the next couple of days might bring, and he definitely wasn't going to imagine lying under the stars with her.

Whatever happened, happened.

That resolved, he picked up their trash and dumped it in a nearby can. As he walked side by side with Shaye down Wild Horse Junction's main street—Wild Horse Way—he was ready for the buggy ride and whatever else came next.

As Shaye drove with Dylan on the byway climbing into the mountains, she felt as if she were seeing everything for the first time. That was crazy, since she'd lived in this area all her life. The huge, uniquely weather-sculptured formations of rock stood in bold relief against the sky. She wondered if she was looking at everything differently because she was with Dylan. Today, the high desert was breathtaking and uplifting in a way she'd never noticed before.

A lump formed in her throat when she realized how Dylan was affecting her world. Could he even guess how his presence in her life was rippling through the whole fabric of it? Sometimes where custody of Timmy was concerned, she felt as if she were consorting with the enemy. Other times, she felt as if they were partners trying to safeguard Timmy's development. And then there were those times when only the two of them existed, bound together by an attraction neither of them understood.

"We're almost there," Dylan said with a glance at her.

"I was surprised when you drove up in this." "This" was a hard-side camper truck. "Where'd you get it?"

"I rented it. I wanted you to be comfortable."

"I didn't think camping was about being comfortable."

"That depends on what kind of camping you do. I love sleeping in tents, but I'm used to fluctuations in temperature, you're not. Tonight, it could drop twenty degrees, maybe more. I didn't want you to shiver all night."

"I think there's another reason you brought a camper."

"Really?"

"Yes, really. A tent could be—" She didn't know quite how to put it. "Claustrophobic. If we don't want this trip to get too intimate, the camper was the better way to go."

His sideways glance lingered on her. "When the temperature drops tonight, we would have no way to stay warm in a tent except by combining our body heat. I didn't want you to think I'd arranged this trip for the wrong reasons."

Dylan's protectiveness bothered her almost as much as her brothers'. She knew as well as he did what would happen if they'd have to share body heat. At least now she was reassured he hadn't intended this as a romantic getaway. Dylan confused her until she didn't know if up was up or down was down.

"I hope your boots are comfortable."

"They are. Gwen, Kylie and I have often gone riding on Saddle Ridge."

"You ride?"

"Don't sound so surprised. I couldn't grow up with somebody like Kylie and not have her teach me a few things about horses. Thanks to her, Gwen and I are both pretty good horsewomen."

"Just when I think I have you figured out, you surprise me."

"Good."

He laughed. "Good?"

"I wouldn't want to be completely predictable. I'd be boring."

"You couldn't be boring if you tried. You're too smart to be boring."

That was a compliment she didn't know how to reply to. So, she remained silent as they passed the turnoff for Devil Canyon and the lookout. Not long after, Dylan veered off the main road onto a narrower one that wound low between two gorges.

"These campsites are protected from the wind. The rock walls are natural barriers."

"I don't suppose cell phones work up here," she commented as they continued downward.

"The truck's equipped with a CB. We can make contact if we have to."

Ten minutes later, Dylan had found the spot he wanted. They drove onto a concrete parking space that seemed to be in the middle of nowhere. High-growing sage brushed against leaves of silvery Russian olive trees. Hopping out, he took a look around and nodded to Shaye. "This looks good. Do you want to try to catch a glimpse of some mustangs? We have about three hours of daylight."

"Sure. Do I need my backpack?"

"You'd better bring it. Make sure you have water and matches."

She could see Dylan's backpack was much heavier than hers. After he motioned toward the west, they started hiking.

"What do you have in there?" she asked, gesturing to his pack.

"Equipment, mostly."

As they walked, Dylan shared bits of history about the mustangs. Shaye also absorbed their surroundings from the low pines growing at their feet to the firs on the distant ridge. In flatter spots she could smell wild onion, glimpse cacti blooming, admire blue larkspur.

Dylan pointed to one of the ridges and kept his voice low. "I want to hike up there in the morning. We'll have a wonderful view of the valley and a couple of the canyons. I'd like to get a start soon after first light. Is that too early for you?"

"There's no reason we can't turn in early," she said with a smile. She thought about them sleeping in the same vicinity.

Dylan's thoughts must have been covering the same territory because his eyes darkened for an instant. Then he turned away from her and kept walking. "Walk in my footsteps if you can. This is rattlesnake territory."

Bears, rattlesnakes and bighorn sheep could be anywhere. Shaye kept close to Dylan.

A short time later he took a pair of binoculars from a case attached to his belt. Stopping, he used them to study areas to the north and the west, then to a valley below.

Suddenly he motioned to her. "Come here."

Without a second thought, she moved toward him.

"Take a look. Over there. Where the rock face forms a vee."

Taking the binoculars, she could see they were the type with a digital camera built in so Dylan could spot his subject and take a picture of it. Finding the area he'd noted, her breath caught. At the base of the cliff, the sun not only shed its light on the rock but on four beautiful mustangs. Sun glanced off the back of a sorrel who was in the company of three other horses—a blue roan, a chestnut foal and another sorrel. They were standing in a circle nibbling at brush.

"They're gorgeous!"

"Aren't they? When they run in the clearings out here, there's not another sight like it."

She watched as one of the larger horses bumped noses with a smaller one, pushing him away from a particular tuft of brush.

"Are they far away from a larger herd?"

"Possibly. But they're their own family. That's a stallion with his mare. The baby looks about a month old. I'd put the second sorrel at about two."

"Kylie wants to adopt a mustang."

"The Bureau of Land Management thins the herds. I know Kylie would probably give one of them a good home, but this is where they belong."

"Loving captivity or freedom. That's a tough choice," Shaye mused.

"Unfortunately, they don't *have* a choice. Man decides for them."

The stallion raised his head and whinnied. He seemed to look straight at them. Then he bobbed his head a few times and the others followed. Suddenly he took off, his tail flying, and led his band into the canyon and out of sight.

Just like that stallion, Shaye was sure Dylan would chose freedom, risk and danger over loving captivity any day.

As she hiked back to their campsite with Dylan, she realized it had been months since she'd physically challenged herself. Timmy had taken up every moment of her time since he was born. Now, she'd have to add her job to that. Yet she still couldn't consider Dylan's offer of financial support. Depending on him was out of the question.

Purple dusk enveloped the mountains as the camper came into view, and she noticed the fire ring.

Unlocking the camper, Dylan lowered the step, went inside and reemerged without his backpack and with a flashlight he clipped on his belt. "I've got about ten minutes until it's completely dark out here. I'm going to collect kindling and wood. You can decide what you want for supper. Perishables are in the icebox. Dry goods are in the cupboard in the corner. I set out a battery-powered lantern so you can see in there."

She didn't like the idea of him stepping away from the campsite for any reason. "Don't go too far, okay?"

With a reassuring smile, he left her.

The inside of the camper wasn't fancy, but rather utilitarian. She saw the bunk above the cab and figured that's where he'd sleep. She'd curl up on the sofa on the left side of the camper. Dylan would never fit there.

The icebox really was an icebox. There was a block of ice inside. On it lay a pack of sandwich meat, cheese and four frozen hamburger patties. She also saw half a dozen eggs stowed on the shelf above the ice with a slab of bacon beside them. When she opened the cupboard, she found cans of baked beans and Harvard beets, a loaf of Italian bread, granola bars, a pack of chocolate cookies, as well as a small frying pan and saucepan. The cans had pop tops and she could see Dylan had thought of everything. Not too little and not too much.

True to his word, Dylan was back in ten minutes and had the fire started before she exited the camper. Going to the truck, he pulled out two sleeping bags from behind the driver's seat.

After he plopped them on the ground, he stood very close to her. "I brought these in case you wanted a taste of sleeping under the stars."

Sleep under the stars with Dylan?

The wind blew over the gorge but they were protected from it. The air was redolent with sage and pine. They'd be open to the elements, yet warm in each other's company. How could all that compare with the inside of the camper?

He ran the back of his hand down the side of her cheek and the caress trembled throughout her whole body.

"You don't have to decide now," he murmured. "You

can always start out here and then when the temperature drops, go inside. Think about it."

Should she live dangerously for a change or head for refuge? If she had any sense, she'd run for safety right now. But standing here, gazing into Dylan's eyes, she couldn't help but want to taste his life.

Was she courageous enough to do that?

Chapter Eleven

The moon, the stars and Dylan.

He motioned to the two sleeping bags. "You can stay zippered up in yours and I'll stay zippered in mine. I don't think you want to miss this."

By "this," she knew he was referring to the wonder of the Wyoming night on a mountain—the scent of wood burning and pine, the hushed majesty of being closer to heaven, the joy of being alive and, for the moment, free of burdens. He was right. She didn't want to miss any of it.

"My jacket's in the truck. I'll get that and be right back."

Shaye couldn't believe how much she enjoyed supper—burgers, beets and chocolate cookies that tasted much better out here than they ever would in her kitchen. Dylan had brought along a five-gallon container of water. Now they used some of that with the biodegradable soap to wash their pans.

After they cleaned up the campsite and a low fire glowed, Shaye pulled her sleeping bag closer to Dylan and climbed inside. The temperature was falling but she was comfortable next to the fire with the insulated fabric enveloping her. Wearing a heavy sweatshirt, Dylan laid on top of his bedroll.

"I suppose you're accustomed to camping out," she commented, just to make conversation.

"Yep. I'm used to pitching a tent and waiting for first light. I don't normally cook when I do it, though."

"You take along freeze-dried rations?"

"I take as little gear as I have to because of the camera equipment. Freeze-dried food is good, so is trail mix or protein bars. Anything I can get hold of that's light to carry."

"How many languages do you speak?" she suddenly asked.

"I've picked up a little of this, a little of that."

"Three, four, five?"

"Each dialect is a language of its own. I'm not fluent in anything, but I can make myself understood."

She had a feeling he was being modest and she liked that about him. He didn't feel a need to shout his accomplishments from every rooftop. There was a quiet confidence about Dylan that gave him strength.

As she propped on her side, facing him, he leaned closer. When he stroked her hair away from her face, she could have purred. The fire cast light and shadows on his features and the intensity in his eyes was mesmerizing as he asked, "Wouldn't you like to see more of the world than Wild Horse Junction? I know you said you're satisfied here, but is being satisfied enough? Don't you want to reach for more?"

After a brief hesitation, she replied, "I reached for more, once. I had dreams of seeing all the continents, but I soon realized the person I'm with is more important than where I go. If I can't be happy in Wild Horse Junction, why do I think I can be happy anywhere? Do you know what I mean?"

The expression on his face told her he did understand. "When I returned to Africa, I guess that's when I realized that no matter where I went, deep inside I wanted to be back here with Timmy."

Her breath caught and the fear that he would take Timmy away must have showed in her eyes.

"Don't," he murmured, slipping down on his side. "Don't be afraid of what I feel for Timmy."

"At any time you could sue for sole custody."

He didn't deny that. "As he gets older, there will be decisions to make. You might need help."

"I'll make them one at a time."

Dylan was so close. He looked so rugged with his windswept hair, beard stubble and sweatshirt. All she had to do was lean slightly toward him and he'd kiss her. Did she truly want that? Did she want *more* than that?

The questions stopped because his eyes seemed to devour her. He didn't make a move yet she felt the inexorable pull toward him. She couldn't keep from tilting her body toward his.

When she did, he said, "I didn't ask you out here to kiss you."

"You didn't ask me out here to count the stars in the sky, either."

With his thumb, he traced the curve of her upper lip. "Would you rather count the stars?"

Slowly she shook her head.

He didn't settle his lips on hers right away. Instead he brushed his nose against hers and kissed each corner of her mouth until she wanted to beg him to just kiss her. After he nibbled her lower lip, tantalizingly slid his tongue along it, finally his arm went around her and he gave her what she wanted—a full, long, deep, wet kiss. The teasing gentleness was gone then and hunger took over.

Dylan's need had so much depth, she drowned in it. It seemed bottomless as he swept her mouth again and again, explored every soft ridge, tasted every sweet crest. Her arms went under his and she held on. She couldn't feel him against her, the sleeping bag was too padded. Mindless with kissing him, she tried to push it down, but it was a barrier that wouldn't go away.

Breaking the kiss, he asked hoarsely, "Do you want to get closer?"

Breathing hard and fast, she knew exactly what he was asking. "Do you have protection?"

"I do," he answered solemnly. "I can zip the two sleeping bags into one, then we can crawl inside to stay warm."

"Just to stay warm?" she asked.

"Whatever happens is up to you, Shaye."

Whatever happens.

Didn't she want to experience again the wonder of making love with him? Didn't she want to feel like a woman? Didn't she want to feel the desire that kept her awake most nights?

The first time she'd made love with Dylan, it had happened so fast and quick. It had been impulsive and reckless. Tonight, she wanted more.

"Let's zip them together," she decided, knowing she was playing with fire and recognizing the danger of it.

It didn't take Dylan long to make two single sleeping bags into a double. He used his sweatshirt and she used her jacket as pillows. After they placed their boots at the foot of the sleeping bag, they lay on their backs, side by side, looking up at the moon and the stars.

"There's Cassiopeia," he pointed out, tracing the stretched-out W.

"I was never very good at picking out the constellations," she murmured. After a few moments she added, "It's so quiet here tonight. I don't hear anything but the fire."

"The sheep are lambing. The bears must have taken the night off," he teased.

Reaching over, he took her hand in his and entwined their fingers. The longer they lay there, the more she was aware of the rise and fall of Dylan's chest, the more she was aware of the heat building inside the sleeping bag, the more she was aware of the need growing inside of her. When she turned her head to look at Dylan, he turned, too. Then they were doing more than looking—they were touching and kissing and holding each other. Never before in her life had she so wanted to be exactly where she was.

When Dylan slid his hands under her sweater, he wasn't in any hurry to rid her of her clothes. His large hands traced circles on her midriff as he kissed her. Hardly able to think, but wanting to give him pleasure, too, she pulled his T-shirt from the waistband of his jeans. Her fingers tunneled underneath. She'd remembered the texture of his skin in her dreams, but it was so much better to be actually touching him now. After he unfastened her bra, he broke the kiss and stroked above her breasts, all the while watching her.

"What?" she asked.

"I want to see if you're enjoying what I'm doing. You've got expressive eyes. They show all, and I think you like what I'm doing now." The tips of his thumbs grazed her nipples and she moaned.

"Oh, yes, I do."

Laughing, he took a nipple between his thumb and forefinger, rolling it, tugging it, making her crazy. She wanted to make him as hot and bothered as he was making her. Sliding one hand from under his T-shirt, she dragged it over his waistband and down his thigh.

This time it was his turn to groan.

"It's getting awfully hot in here," he complained, and she laughed. But she didn't stop. She wanted to see how far she could go before Dylan's restraint broke. As she cupped him and molded her hand to him, she knew he was fully aroused. But Dylan had more stamina and self-control than she ever expected, although he had to want satisfaction as badly as she did. He unfastened her jeans and slid one hand under the waistband, teasing around the edge of her panties.

"Your skin's so silky," he murmured in her ear as he kissed her neck, pushed her sweater to the side and kissed her shoulder, too.

"Your skin's so hot."

"That's not all that's hot."

He moved, putting his legs between hers and settled his knee right where she wanted him to touch her.

"Dylan," she breathed.

"What?" He moved his knee in a gentle pressure that created tension inside of her. After he pulled down her zipper, he shifted his knee and slipped his hand into her panties.

"Look at me," he ordered gently.

Her cheeks had to be red. She was embarrassed and felt shy, but she looked at him, anyway. Embarrassment fled as his finger performed magic. Her cry rang out into the black night as she climaxed sharply, quickly, the trembling orgasm taking her totally by surprise.

As the quivering sensation ended, he said, "I can't wait to sink inside of you."

He threw the cover aside for a short while until they undressed each other. The night air cooled their heated skin, but not enough to cool their ardor.

"Stretch out in the middle," he suggested, and after Shaye did that, he slipped on a condom and lowered himself on top of her, pulling the sleeping bag over his back. When he touched her, he found her still damp and ready for him. Slowly he slid inside.

"Have you ever done anything like this before?" She studied him, needing to know.

"You mean, made love with a woman on a mountain?" He didn't look angry, but rather amused, and she nodded.

"No, I haven't. Most women prefer mattresses and amenities."

"I'm not most women."

"You've done this before?" he asked with a chuckle.

"Goodness, no. I can't believe I'm doing it now."

"You're doing it, Shaye. You're doing it."

Their banter faded away into sighs and moans. Dylan's thrusts were strong and hard, and Shaye welcomed every one of them. She'd climaxed and never expected to have it happen again, but that delicious tension began winding tight inside her once more. Her muscles tightened, her legs gripped Dylan and she thought she heard the thundering hooves of a thousand mustangs. The sound was simply the blood rushing through her, faster, hotter, until she was crying out once more and Dylan's groan resonated through her.

A few moments later Dylan's beard stubble grazed her cheek as he lifted his head and looked down at her. "Are you all right?"

Still wrapped in the haze of desire, she nodded. In Dylan's arms, she felt very all right.

"I think we'll go inside to sleep. You'll be more comfortable."

"I don't think I can move." A delicious lethargy had taken her over.

"You don't have to move. I will." Before she could protest, he'd separated from her. She felt the rush of cold air as he moved away from her and the bedroll. Then he scooped her up with the sleeping bag, and she wrapped her arms around his neck. "What are you doing?"

"Taking you to the camper."

"You're naked. You don't have shoes on."

When he laughed, she felt like an idiot, but his voice was tender as he replied, "I'm fine. By the time you snuggle up in bed, I'll have the fire out and I'll be in there with you."

They'd left the door of the camper open and now he shoved it aside with his elbow and deposited her inside. Climbing into the bunk above the cab, she let the sleeping bag drop to the floor. There was a sheet and a blanket already in the bunk and she used those. A few minutes later she felt the camper rock slightly as Dylan stepped inside. He must have brought their clothes in because she heard the rustle of fabric and shoes clunk on the floor. Then he was beside her, adjusting the sheet and blanket over his lower body.

The covers were cool and she shivered.

"Turn on your side," he murmured, "with your back to me."

After she did, Dylan warmed her. As his arm went around her, she knew she wouldn't be cold again. She closed her eyes and Dylan's breath was warm on her neck. Sleep came easily, and relaxing into Dylan's embrace, Shaye knew she'd never felt so safe.

* * *

Morning dawned and sun streamed in the small camper window. As Shaye awakened, she felt Dylan's arm still around her and she kept very still. Last night had been wonderful. He'd loved her so well...so tenderly. Yet doubts began to take the place of sated well-being.

Vivid memories from last night came flooding back, and she considered every one of them as if she were reading one of her case reports. Supposedly, sex hadn't been Dylan's motivation in bringing her up here. But when she examined the whole picture, hadn't each of his words, each touch, each look led to that? Did he think if they were lovers she wouldn't go forward with Timmy's adoption? Did he think if they were lovers she wouldn't oppose what he wanted to do? And what was that, exactly? Have Timmy live with him when he was around? Live with her when he wasn't? She simply couldn't imagine it, and now in the light of day the idea that Dylan was using her in some way simply wouldn't go away.

She was to start back to work a week from tomorrow. Did he want her to leave Timmy with him rather than with Barb? What happened when she had to work full-time and Dylan was gone? She wanted Timmy's life to be consistent and stable.

If she brought up any of her doubts now, she had the feeling the whole day would be tense. It seemed better to wait. Maybe they could talk after they got back to camp...after he photographed the horses. She had one question she had to ask him, and she didn't know if she wanted to hear the answer to it. She had the day to think about it, and to put last night in perspective.

Dylan's hand moved on her hip. In a husky voice, he asked, "Are you awake?"

She turned onto her back. "Yes, I'm awake."

As she studied his face, she realized she was more in love with him than she ever thought possible. But she wasn't sure about Dylan's emotions any more than his motives. And she couldn't let him kiss her again, she couldn't let him touch her again until she sorted everything out.

She motioned to the sunshine dappling the floor. "It looks like it's going to be a great day." Sitting up, she scooted to the edge of the mattress and stepped down onto the camper floor. "I'll wash up and brush my teeth, then we can scramble up those eggs. Do you want the bacon, too?"

The sleep-hazy hooded look was gone from Dylan's eyes as he studied her now. "You're chipper this morning."

"I can't wait to see the horses again. How are we going to find them?"

Picking up his clothes from the sofa, she sorted them into one pile and hers into another.

"Either we'll find them, or they'll find us."

"They'll find us? Aren't they afraid of humans?"

"That depends. Julia and I found out if we tried to hide and pretend we weren't there, they were more skittish—as if they expected a predator to pop out at them at any moment. I often got a better view when we just stood perfectly still, or sat perfectly still, out in the open. Then they seemed to pay us no more mind than a tree. I'm not sure how they think. It would be interesting to study them over a period of time."

He climbed down from the bunk. "We might see more foals. Mares have babies through November."

"Have you done research on the wild mustangs?" she asked, wondering how he knew all this.

"No, but I came up here anytime I could when I was a kid."

"And you photographed them before?"

"Not really. For some reason when I'd come up here to watch them, I'd forget about taking pictures. I'd get caught up in their antics."

"I hope we can find them."

"We will."

When Dylan smiled at her like that, everything inside her responded to him. That was what she didn't want today. While they were talking, she'd quickly dressed, not wanting to be naked in front of him now. She felt too vulnerable.

Putting on her hiking boots, but not lacing them, she went to the door.

"I can heat water so you can wash up."

He seemed oblivious to his nakedness. She wasn't. "No need. I know you want to get going. I'm just going outside for a few minutes while...while you get dressed."

"If you want to stay in here and use the portable potty first, I can start breakfast."

The truth was, she couldn't be cooped up in the camper with him a moment longer. She couldn't look at all that tanned skin, his fit body... "No, you go ahead and give a shout when you're done."

Opening the door, she stepped outside into the sage-filled, sun-streaked, blue-skied morning, needing a hefty, healthy dose of fresh air.

The band stallion protected his mares and the two foals, ambling around them. Dylan knew the dun-colored horse was aware they were there. But as long as the animals sensed no danger, they didn't seem to mind. At one point, the stallion headed for them, snorted, then changed direction and veered away from them. Earlier, he and Shaye had seen a group of bachelors, young stallions not old enough to rule over their own band. When they matured, they would vie for the right to steal a mare.

Today, everything was peaceful...at least in the mustang world.

He and Shaye had taken a break and eaten lunch a bit earlier. She'd been terribly quiet this morning and he knew something was on her mind because she shied away whenever he got close. He wished he knew what was running through her pretty head.

Lowering his camera from his eye, he checked his watch. "We should probably start back if we want to be home by supper."

"Yes, we should," Shaye agreed. After taking a long last look at the wild mustangs, she said, "Thank you for this. I really enjoyed it."

There was genuine pleasure in her voice but her words were much too polite.

As they began the hike back to camp, the sun was hot on his shoulders, the wind stiff through his hair. He'd told Shaye to bring a hat, knowing she wasn't used to the sun. With the straw hat plunked on her head, its tie under her chin, she looked adorable. She'd tied her jacket around her waist as he'd done with his sweat-shirt. As they trekked over rock, hiked over brush, stopped now and then to take in blooming cacti and wildflowers as well as another beautiful vista, his adren-aline surged faster.

"The gallery showing is Saturday night. Think you'll be able to come?" he asked.

"Sure. I wouldn't miss it. Flutes and Drums will be the hottest spot in town. With the tourist traffic, you should sell all your photographs."

"We'll see. Lily's trying to convince me to put more time into marketing prints."

"Signed and numbered ones?" Shaye asked.

"Yes. That would make them more collectible."

"That sounds like a plan."

Shaye's pablum-like response made Dylan stop and catch her elbow. "Tell me what's wrong. You've been distracted all morning."

After a look at her boots, she raised her gaze to his. "I was going to wait until we got back to camp."

"Wait for what?"

"I need answers. I need to know what last night was all about."

"That's easy. It was about you and me enjoying each other."

"I don't have affairs, Dylan. I don't date a man, sleep with him and then move on as if it never happened."

He'd thought they were getting to know each other better. He'd thought she'd finally stopped denying the chemistry between them so they could connect on a deeper level. But now he wasn't so sure. Now he realized he'd been right about Shaye, and she might want something he couldn't give her.

"What do you want to know, Shaye?" He didn't know what he expected, but the question she asked wasn't it.

"Tell me something, Dylan. If Julia hadn't made me Timmy's legal guardian, if you'd met me here or on some photo shoot, would you have slept with me?"

As he absorbed her question, it made him angry. "That's a hypothetical situation. I can't answer that."

"You can't or you won't? Face it, Dylan. I'm probably not the kind of woman you usually get involved with, am I?"

When he thought about the women he'd been involved with in the past, he knew she was right. He chose women who weren't interested in any more than satisfaction and comfort for a few nights. He chose women who didn't have strings attached, who wouldn't tie him down.

"I can't classify women into Type A and Type B—"

"Yes, you can. Who were you last involved with?"

"You want her name?"

"No. What did she *do?*"

"She was a reporter," he answered in exasperation.

"Right. On assignment in a place where you were staying for a limited amount of time."

"Yes," he snapped.

"See what I mean? So, why me? Because you think it will make our road a little smoother? Because you think I won't go to a lawyer again?"

"You think I slept with you to keep you under my control?" If he hadn't been angry before, he was now. He'd never met anyone like Shaye. He'd never been attracted to anyone in the way he was attracted to her. No, she wasn't his usual type. Whatever was going on was potent and damn confusing.

But he knew one thing and he knew it well. "Sleeping with you had *nothing* to do with Timmy."

As the wind rushed over canyons, bent the brim on Shaye's hat and whistled through the tree line, time seemed to stand still.

Finally she replied, "I wish I could believe that."

Her attitude and her doubts were a problem he couldn't solve on his own. He was sure of that now and it added to his anger—at himself, at her, at the whole situation. "Nothing I say is going to affect what you think."

When she didn't deny that, he stepped away from her and turned toward camp. They were back at square one and damned if he knew how to proceed now.

Chapter Twelve

On Saturday night, Flutes and Drums was alive with gallery shoppers, Native American flute music and small groups speaking intimately about Dylan's photographs. Most of the space had been transformed into a showcase for his work. As Shaye studied one picture after the next, she was struck by color, design and a style that set Dylan Malloy apart. The most dramatic works were those taken in the Serengetti and Antarctica...but then she spotted a few of the wild mustangs that shouted freedom and those were just as captivating. When she finally stood in front of Julia's display, tears came to her eyes. The shots of his sister were magnificent. They captured her spirit, her sparkling eyes, her love for life.

"What do you think?"

The deep voice was close to her shoulder. It resonated through her, shaking her up and exciting her. Their drive home from the mountains had been tense, though Dylan had mentioned he'd be working at the gallery this week, helping Lily sort and hang the pictures for the show. He'd visited Timmy three evenings and had bathed him without Shaye's help. They'd exchanged polite conversation, but Dylan hadn't asked if she was coming tonight. She hadn't been sure she should.

But she had, and here they were.

Although sometimes she wasn't certain of Dylan's motives, she was sure of one thing. "You knew your sister, and it shows."

He was quiet for a moment. "I like to think I did. I hope she knows how proud I am of her and the life she made."

"She knows."

There was a sign near the display of Julia's pictures that told gallery-goers the portraits were unavailable for purchase.

"Have you seen everything?" he asked, studying her carefully.

"Not that corner over there." She pointed to an area that was the most secluded in the gallery.

"I'll walk you over."

As they crossed the room, Shaye relived the night they'd spent in the camper as well as the first time they'd made love. Was she altogether wrong that he wanted to use her? Had her dad's lack of attention and taking her for granted set up a distrust of men? Chad's departure from her life and the way it happened had just cemented the idea that she was better off on her own.

Walking beside Dylan, remembering being held by him, she wanted to believe she didn't have to be alone. Not in raising Timmy and not living her life. Even if Dylan's attentions weren't fueled by the desire to control her and manipulate her, was he the type of man to stay? His sister had said he wasn't, and Julia had believed he'd never want to be tied down.

They were a few feet away from the display when Shaye recognized the object of Dylan's photographic skill—Timmy.

Again there was a small sign stating the works in this display couldn't be purchased. As she studied the photographs, she could read the feeling behind them just as she could in Julia's portraits. Dylan loved his nephew, that was so easy to see. Most of the shots were close-ups of a happy baby, a frowning baby, a delighted baby. There was one in particular that she liked—Timmy's christening hat tilted sideways on his head. He had one finger shoved into his mouth and he looked like a mischievous little angel.

"How do you do it?" she asked.

"Do what?"

"Manage to capture the perfect moment."

"I don't always do that," he replied. "Especially not with you. If I did, you wouldn't think I was going to run off with Timmy and leave you behind."

She never expected him to bring this up here. "We can't talk now."

"No, we can't," Dylan agreed, as a tall thin man in

a perfectly cut suit crossed to Dylan and put his hand on his shoulder. Up close, she could see lines on his face she hadn't noticed from farther away. He was much older than his fit frame and his energetic gait indicated.

"I just spoke to Lily, and you, my boy, are practically sold out. Those blue dots on each photograph mean money in your pocket. We'll have to talk about which ones you want to make into prints."

Instead of commenting on what the man had said, Dylan introduced him to Shaye. "Shaye, this is my agent, Dan Ortez. Dan, this is Shaye Bartholomew."

The agent pumped Shaye's hand vigorously. "I was hoping I'd meet you. Dylan's told me how good you are with Timmy." He nodded to the display. "Those pictures are the talk of the night. You could sell each and every one of them," he said to Dylan and added, "for a couple of reasons. Because of your name and your talent, but also because they're so damn appealing."

"Not for sale."

"You know, if all my clients were as stubborn as you, I'd quit representing them. I have another African deal for you…and one in Antarctica later in the year. We can talk about them tomorrow over breakfast before I leave. *Wildlife Review* needs an answer by the end of the week and the African photos by September first."

"I didn't have plans to leave Wild Horse this summer."

When he shot a glance at Shaye, she had no idea what he was thinking. Did he not want to leave to spend time with Timmy? To spend time with her? To make sure she didn't start adoption proceedings?

"We'll talk about it in the morning," Ortez assured Dylan, and clapped him on the back. "Congratulations again. You really should have some of that champagne the waiter is circulating. It's first-rate, and so is Lily Reynolds. I think you've made a good choice in having her distribute your work."

As Ortez moved away, silence settled between them. Finally, Dylan said, "I'd like to take Timmy tomorrow afternoon."

"Take him?"

"Yes. I'd like to take him to my place, let him get used to it, spend some guy-time with him."

She'd known this day was coming…Dylan had hinted at it before. She also knew if she said no, Dylan would go to court.

"I start work Monday morning. I'd like to be with him tomorrow evening."

"That's fine. Why don't I pick him up after my breakfast with Dan? I'll keep him until around five. You can have the afternoon to do whatever you want."

Dylan was making it sound as if she should be grateful for the break. In reality, Timmy had become such a part of her that whenever she was away from him or whenever he was away from her, she missed him.

"You're just going to keep him at your apartment?" she asked.

"If I were going to take him anywhere else, I'd tell you."

Dylan's jaw had tightened and as she looked at his mouth, she remembered his kisses, remembered his touches, remembered everything that had made her fall in love with him.

"*There* you are," boomed a voice she recognized immediately.

As she turned, she saw her father coming toward her, Nicole Taylor beside him.

"Your brother told me you'd be here and I thought it would be a good place to introduce you to Nicole. Nicole, this is my daughter, Shaye." Then, waving to all of Dylan's pictures, he pronounced, "Good stuff, Malloy. Nicole, this is the photographer."

Nicole Taylor was a pretty woman. She had blond curly hair that was fixed on top of her head. Wearing a red halter-top dress, she'd stand out in a crowd.

With a friendly smile, Nicole extended her hand to Shaye. "Hi, it's good to finally meet you. You, too, Mr. Malloy."

Carson said, "Why don't you ask Mr. Malloy about that picture you want to buy? It hasn't been sold yet but it will be soon if you don't claim it."

"Which one are you interested in?" Dylan asked politely.

"The kangaroos touching noses. That is just *too* cute."

As Dylan and Nicole moved away, Dylan glanced at Shaye, relaying the message that their conversation wasn't finished. She knew that. She also knew that if Dylan left for that shoot in Africa, he'd probably take the one in Antarctica, too, then another after that. Just how important had Timmy become to him? How important was *she* to him?

She had more pride than to fall into an affair whenever he returned home.

"Randall told me you saw me and Nicole together at Horse and Buggy Days," her father began.

"Yes, I did. Why didn't you tell me you were dating someone?"

He shrugged. "I wasn't sure I was. We went for coffee a few times. I want you to get to know her."

Her father's voice had taken on that authoritarian tone he'd always used with her. "Is that an order?"

Carson looked taken aback. "You can't tell me you don't like her. You've just met her!"

"I didn't say I don't like her, but you think ordering me to get to know her will establish a friendship between us?"

"I don't know what's gotten into you, Shaye. You used to be so—"

"Obedient? That's when I was a child. I always did what you asked, when you asked it. But if you want me to get to know Nicole, you can't just demand it. You have to help facilitate it. You have to be around for more than two minutes. I've got to ask again. Why didn't you tell me you were dating her? It's obvious Randall and John knew, but not me."

Although her father looked chagrined, he replied honestly, "I didn't know how you'd react."

"So, you didn't bother to tell me. But now that I've caught up with your life, everything's supposed to be all right?"

"See? I knew you'd be upset."

"I'm not upset you're dating a woman twenty-five years younger than you. I'm not upset you're dating. I am upset that you've never tried to foster a relationship between *us*."

This was not the place to have this conversation,

either, she realized, but she never seemed to see her father anymore. It wasn't as if she could drop in on him at home. He was never there.

"Of course, we have a relationship. I'm your father."

"We have DNA in common, Dad. I'm not sure about anything else. Do you know anything about my life? You've never even held Timmy. Are you going to ignore the fact that he's your grandson?"

"He's *not* my grandson. If you get attached to that baby, you're going to get hurt. Dylan Malloy has money and influence, too. He's the boy's uncle. If he wants the baby, he won't let you keep him. If you get too attached—"

"I'm already attached. I love him as if I gave birth to him, and *I'm* the one with legal custody." She sighed and tried as she'd tried many times before. "Maybe you and I should have dinner sometime and we can talk about it."

"You know my schedule," he snapped.

"Yes, I do. You've always had that kind of schedule and that's why we've never gotten to know each other."

Carson Bartholomew looked speechless, which was a first for him. Before either of them could take a step to bridge the gap between them, Nicole was beside Carson again, tucking her hand into the crook of his arm.

"I bought it. I now own a Dylan Malloy original."

"Wonderful," Carson exclaimed, all of his attention on his date, as if he'd forgotten the conversation he and Shaye had just had. "Now, why don't we go have some of that champagne and a few hors d'oeuvres? Then we can go over to Clementine's and dance for a while."

Clementine's had a live band every Saturday night. Shaye didn't think her father had ever set foot in the place, but now his life was changing and she wondered if he was one of those men who would consider starting a second family. If he did, maybe he'd find the happiness and contentment that had always seemed to elude him...that he'd never stopped and tried to find.

To Shaye he said, "When we were at Clementine's last weekend, Nicole taught me a new dance. That's great exercise." As her father moved away, he said, "I'll give you a call."

How many times had her father promised that, but the phone had never rung? If he didn't call her, she'd try to call him. She didn't want the distance between them to grow any greater. Every time she reached out to him, she hoped he'd reach back. Usually she got hurt hoping.

After her father and Nicole walked away, Dylan strode to her. However, someone across the room called to him.

"How long are you going to stay?" he asked.

"I've got to get back home."

"I probably won't get out of here before midnight."

She hated this awkwardness between them that nothing they could say or do seemed to dispel. Maybe the problem was that they'd done too much and had become intimate when they should have simply remained coparents.

"I'll see you tomorrow," she said quietly.

He nodded, then walked away to join Lily, who was speaking with a few of his admirers. Shaye felt as if she had one foot in Dylan's life and one foot out of it. She felt as if he had one foot in her life and one foot out of it.

Tomorrow afternoon she'd have to keep busy.

Very busy.

When Shaye arrived at Saddle Ridge Ranch on Sunday afternoon, she knew something was wrong. Call it a sixth sense...or just being observant...or just knowing Kylie. Trying to forget about Dylan taking Timmy to his apartment, she studied her surroundings. Sunday was always a quieter day on the ranch, not that chores still didn't have to be done. Dix usually spent the morning doing a few chores but then left. Kylie, on the other hand, used Sunday as her catch-up day. That meant working horses she hadn't had time to work during the week. It often meant riding to the north ridge to check cattle or just cleaning tack. But whatever Kylie chose to do, she usually did it around the barn. Today, however, all was quiet...much too quiet. The big barn door was shut and so was the side door. There weren't any horses turned out in the pasture.

Something was definitely wrong.

After Shaye parked, she walked to the house and climbed the steps. On this beautiful early July day, the heavy wood door was closed. That wasn't like Kylie, either. Shaye might think the place was deserted, but she'd parked beside Kylie's small blue pickup.

Opening the screen door, she knocked hard. After a few silent moments, she knocked again.

When Kylie came to the door, Shaye knew immediately something had happened. Her friend's eyes were red and Shaye could see she'd been crying.

"What's happened? Are you okay? Is the baby okay?"

Slowly, Kylie opened the door wider. "Alex left."

Following Kylie inside, Shaye went with her to the living room. "What do you mean, he left?"

"There's a rodeo in Las Vegas. He wasn't supposed to leave until Tuesday."

Sitting beside her friend on the sofa, Shaye asked, "Why did he leave early?"

Kylie looked stricken. "Because he didn't want to hear what I had to say. He doesn't want to face everything that has to be done around here. He believes Dix and I can handle it, and we can't. Not now."

"Did you tell him about the baby?"

Now spots of color dotted Kylie's cheeks. "Oh, yes. And you know what he said? He thinks I got pregnant to hold him here more. He won't go to counseling with me. All he wants to do is ride bulls, and that's just not good enough any longer."

"What are you going to do?"

"That's what I've been thinking about ever since Alex left this morning. I feel I have a responsibility to Saddle Ridge, to Dix, to the animals here, even to Alex's dad's memory. But I have an even bigger responsibility now to our baby." She protectively laid her hand over her tummy.

"Maybe Alex will come around. Maybe this child will make him realize the responsibility he has."

"I think we both know Alex runs from responsibility rather than accepts it. *I* have to accept that fact now. But I can't give up without giving him a chance. He'll be gone about two weeks. Mr. Tompkins offered me the job in his agency and I'm going to take it. I need money coming in for all the things this baby will need."

"Do you have health insurance?"

Sadly, Kylie shook her head. "It's just too expensive. So I have to save money in the next few months for that, too. I'm going to have a talk with Dix when he gets back tonight. He doesn't know I'm pregnant yet. If, by the time Alex gets home, his attitude hasn't changed, then I'm going to have to leave."

Shaye dropped her arm around her friend's shoulders. It was about time Alex Warner faced up to the mess he'd gotten himself into. It was about time he faced the fact that Kylie couldn't handle Saddle Ridge and a baby on her own.

"Where will you go if you leave?"

"I checked in town and Madge Branson still rents rooms above the Silver Dollar. She said she'd give me a monthly rate and if I help her with her books, she'll discount that."

"You could stay with me and save the money you'd spend on a room."

"Thank you," Kylie said. "You know I appreciate the offer. But I have to get myself together and stand on my own two feet."

"Maybe so, but the offer still stands."

Shaking her head and taking a deep breath, her friend gave her a half-smile. "If you want a roommate, maybe you should ask Dylan Malloy."

"That would solve *nothing*," Shaye murmured.

"In the matter of custody with Timmy, or between the two of you?"

"How did you know—"

"That you're involved? Oh, Shaye. It's *so* obvious when the two of you are together."

"Exactly *what's* obvious?"

"That you've been together."

Shaye's expression must have been so amazed that Kylie laughed. "Well, haven't you been together?"

Finally, Shaye answered. "Yes."

Picking up a throw pillow on the sofa, Kylie hugged it to her. "A man and woman are different around each other once they've been intimate. Everything changes. It's in the way Dylan looks at you and you look at him."

"I didn't come here to talk about Dylan."

"Didn't you?"

"No. There's an offer on the table for him to go back to Africa. If he does, I can stop worrying about him suing for custody and adopting Timmy. I can go ahead with the adoption myself."

"Do you want him to leave?"

That was the irony. If Dylan left, she'd be free to mother her son. But if Dylan left, her heart would go with him.

"Actually, I came out here this afternoon to forget about Dylan Malloy. Have you had lunch yet?"

"No."

"Let's raid the refrigerator then go for a walk. It will do us both a lot of good." When Kylie looked doubtful, Shaye stood. "I'll tell you all about seeing the mustangs in the canyons."

"You went to the Big Horns?"

"Yep."

"With Dylan?"

"With Dylan. But we're going to talk about the horses, not Dylan."

A smile played on Kylie's lips again. "Whatever you say."

"I only wish," Shaye muttered as Kylie rose to her feet, too, and Shaye accompanied her to the kitchen.

At five o'clock on the dot, Dylan returned Timmy to Shaye. When she opened her door, there he was, smiling, holding the baby and his diaper bag in which she'd packed all his paraphernalia.

Starting inside, Dylan explained, "He took about a half hour nap around one. He's been awake since then but he hasn't been fussy. Before we left, I diapered and fed him, so he might go down for a nap now."

As she lifted Timmy from Dylan, Shaye brought him close, nuzzled her nose in his hair and kissed his baby cheek. He waved his arms and gooed at her, and her heart felt a hundred times lighter. Dylan had taken good care of him and she had to accept the fact that he was a great hands-on dad.

"Did you do anything exciting?" she asked lightly.

Her casual use of the word brought a more-than-casual look into Dylan's eyes. He knew excitement and so did she when they were in each other's arms. "I can keep a journal when I have Timmy," he joked. Yet she could tell he was trying to keep everything easy between them, too.

"That's not necessary."

"I showed him a picture of a cougar, a cheetah and a jaguar, and tried to teach him the difference."

"You didn't."

"Sure did. I might as well start now."

At her shoulder, Timmy looked sleepy. "I'm going to take him upstairs to his crib. He's almost outgrowing this portable one in the living room." She needed to catch her breath and get a little distance from Dylan.

Fifteen minutes later, she was so engrossed in talking to Timmy, asking him about his afternoon, playing with his fingers and settling him in his crib that she didn't hear Dylan come up the steps.

She saw him when she started the music box on Timmy's mobile.

Standing in the doorway, looking relaxed and sexy in a red shirt, jeans and sneakers, he wasn't a man to be ignored. "I bought a couple of those videotapes for babies. He seemed to watch one of them for a while."

"I've heard about them but I haven't gotten any yet," Shaye admitted, crossing to him slowly.

He didn't move from the doorway. "There's something we need to get straight."

"What?" she asked softly.

"I didn't take you camping to seduce you. Once we were lying side by side, I couldn't resist the fire between us and neither could you. What happened had nothing to do with Timmy, nothing to do with whether you have custody or I have custody. I wanted to be with you, Shaye. I think you want to be with me, too, but you're fighting it for all you're worth."

Slowly she shook her head. "I'm not very good at living in the moment."

"Maybe you just need practice. Maybe you just need to trust your instincts and trust mine."

"Dylan, I—"

"And you've *got* to stop thinking," he admonished her, slipping his hand to the ribbon in her hair, untying it, letting her hair fall to her shoulders.

"I don't think when you're touching me. That's the problem."

With a chuckle, he deliberately put his fingers under her hair, angled them upward and ran his thumb along her chin. "So, you're not thinking right now?"

"This isn't good for either of us."

"I don't agree." Suddenly he dropped his hand to his side. "It's your decision. I can go if that's what you want."

When Dylan kissed her and caressed her, when he made love to her as if she were the most desirable woman in the world, she almost believed she was. If she made love with Dylan again, that's exactly what she'd be doing—making love.

How many more regrets would she have? How many wonderful memories would she have if he stayed in Wild Horse Junction?

A little voice inside her head whispered, *Men like Dylan don't stay.*

This time she didn't listen to the voice. This time she made a conscious decision to live in the moment. This time she was fully aware that she was risking everything because she loved this man so much.

"I don't want you to go."

"You want me to stay for supper?" he teased, and she realized that this time she had to tell him what she wanted. This time he wouldn't sweep her away, not unless it was a conscious decision on her part to let him.

"I want you to stop me from thinking. I want to feel you inside me. I want you to hold me until Timmy needs me again."

If they were lucky, they had about an hour, maybe a little more.

When Dylan hungrily covered her lips with his, she realized that when she was away from him, she missed him. When she was away from him, she felt restless. When she was away from him, she felt…alone. Since February she'd thought her feelings about Dylan revolved around Timmy. But that wasn't true and she knew it now.

She didn't hold back as Dylan deepened the kiss. As he swept her into his arms and carried her to her bedroom, she held on. She had to hold on now because later he might be gone.

Tomorrow he might be gone.

The thoughts stopped as Dylan undressed her and caressed her. Only feeling remained.

It was enough for now.

Chapter Thirteen

On Thursday Shaye went to work and felt changed. For so long her work had been the focus of her life. Then Julia had left her a precious gift and her world revolved around a baby. Now her world revolved around Timmy...*and* Dylan.

Her practical self was telling her she was *so* in trouble and she'd never get out of it. The problem was, she didn't *want* to get out of it. At the beginning of the week, after Dylan met her at Barb's to pick up Timmy, they'd gone to her place for lunch, played with Timmy until nap time, then made love. They'd spent the whole day together on Tuesday, the Fourth of July. Both nights he'd stayed with her and she loved the intimacies they'd shared.

Today, however, her instincts were telling her something was wrong. Dylan had phoned yesterday to tell her he was working. She understood "working." Yet something in his voice—distance, maybe—had alerted her that more than work was involved. Maybe he didn't want to become too committed.

Maybe he was thinking about taking the assignment in Africa. Maybe being a dad was on his agenda, but not being tied down by a woman.

Last night, Timmy had been awake on and off, and Shaye hadn't gotten much sleep. Maybe she was imagining things.

When she picked up Timmy at Barb's, her sister-in-law pointed to the half-empty bottles on the counter. "He didn't eat as much as usual."

Shaye felt Timmy's face and hands, but he was cool to the touch. "I'll take his temperature when I get him home."

"It could just be that he wasn't hungry. We have days like that, too," Barb reassured her with a smile.

"Yes, I guess we do. Is it all right if I drop him off a half hour earlier tomorrow?"

"Sure. You know I'm up. Something unusual at work?"

"I jumped right back in."

"A special case taking up most of your time?"

"Actually, there is. Did you read in the paper about the little girl who was left alone?"

"Yes, I remember that. At the time I tried to understand the mind-set of the woman who would do that. I just couldn't. Is the mother terrifically young? I suppose that could account for bad judgment."

"She's twenty and she's back. That's what the extra meetings are all about. I'm going to be out of the office most of the morning and you won't be able to reach me on my cell phone. We have an appearance before a judge and I'll have to have my phone turned off."

"I can leave a message, though, can't I?"

"Sure. If you do, I'll get back to you as soon as I can. I might be a little late picking Timmy up. Is that a problem?"

"Now, where else would I be but here?"

Although Shaye smiled, she insisted, "I want you to tell me if you mind."

"I don't mind one bit. I miss not having a baby in my arms. In fact, I've been having a discussion with Randall about the possibility of having another child."

"Discussing?" Shaye asked teasingly.

Her sister-in-law's cheeks reddened a bit. "Yes, well, I guess we have gone past discussing. I stopped my birth control last week. I'm so excited I feel like a newlywed again."

"I'm sure Randall appreciates that."

Both of them laughed.

"He sure does," Barb confided. "I didn't know how he'd feel about going through the diaper stage again since we're way out of that now. But I think he wants to postpone having an empty nest as long as I do."

Timmy had begun wriggling in Shaye's arms. Kissing his forehead, she said, "Okay, big boy. Let's go home."

"Is Dylan coming over this afternoon?"

"He didn't say. I know he's working on an article and he has a deadline on it."

"He's really good with Timmy. He's not afraid to get his hands dirty. I haven't seen him back away once from anything baby-related. Or is he just putting on a good show for me?"

"No, Dylan isn't like that." Over the past few days, she'd stopped questioning his motives. Over the past few days, she'd tumbled head over heels more in love with him.

By the time Shaye gave Timmy his bath that evening, she wondered if Dylan was still working. Her phone rang as she laid Timmy in his crib and started his mobile. As if he'd read her mind, Dylan said, "Hi, there. Sorry I didn't call sooner, but I got caught up in what I was doing and forgot the time."

"What *were* you doing?"

There was only a slight hesitation. "I was reformatting the mustang shots, and I had a few international calls to make. With the time difference, I didn't have much leeway on when I had to make them."

"I understand," she said, and she did. She knew Dylan wasn't used to accounting for his time. "Do you want to come over for a nightcap?" She asked the question lightly, wanting to know if there was something bothering him, if there was a reason she hadn't seen him since Tuesday.

"I'd like that," he said, sounding as if he meant it. "But I have to finish the copy on some photos and journal entries."

"Journal entries?"

"I keep a journal when I'm on a shoot—descriptions, names of places, that kind of thing. Anyway, I have to fax this in the morning."

With her pride taking center stage now, she didn't ask

him what he was going to be doing this weekend, though she wanted to. Had he already had enough? Was he tired of her?

"Why don't you go, then," she murmured. "Good luck with your article."

"I'll see you sometime tomorrow," he assured her. "Then we can make definite plans."

"All right." She wanted to say she missed him, but that wouldn't be a good idea at all.

When she hung up the phone, tears pricked in her eyes, but she blinked them away, went to stand at Timmy's crib and gave her son another good-night kiss.

To Shaye's relief, Timmy slept through the night. Friday morning was overcast as she went to his room when she heard him crying. She saw at once that his nose was running. When she took his temperature with the ear thermometer, it registered at ninety-nine point eight. She could expect a low-grade fever might accompany a cold.

Forty-five minutes later, she was standing in Barb's living room, not at all sure she should leave for work.

"He'll be fine," Barb assured her. "Babies get colds. Go to work. When you get out of court, give me a call and I'll give you an update."

Although Shaye left Timmy with her sister-in-law, she had an uneasy feeling in her chest. But she told herself there was nothing she could do if she stayed home with Timmy. The cold would have to run its course.

By noon, Dylan swore in frustration. Shaye wasn't answering her cell phone. With her incommunicado, he decided to stop at Barb's to see Timmy and to find out if Shaye just wasn't answering *his* messages. He'd had work to do and that had caused a strain between them. He'd never had to be concerned about unorthodox hours before because he'd never had a serious involvement.

Was his involvement with Shaye serious?

When Barb opened her door, he could hear Timmy crying and Shaye's sister-in-law looked upset.

"What's wrong?"

"Timmy's coughing now and wheezing slightly. I can't get hold of Shaye because she's at the courthouse. I was about to take Timmy's temperature."

So, that was why he couldn't reach Shaye. Moving inside the house with Barb, Dylan went to the crib she had set up in one corner of the family room. "Let's take it," he said.

After she read the ear thermometer, Barb paled. "It's one hundred and three."

"Did Shaye leave a list of emergency numbers?"

"Yes, I have them on the refrigerator."

Dylan hurried to get it himself. Taking his cell phone from his pocket, he dialed the number for Dr. Carrera's office. Although he was a neonatologist, he followed his little patients until they were six months old, then transferred them to a pediatrician. Dylan was glad Dr. Carrera knew Timmy's history. "We have to call Shaye's supervisor. There's got to be somebody who can get a message to her."

While the phone line at the doctor's office rang, Dylan prayed the man was available, prayed whatever was wrong with Timmy wasn't as serious as he thought.

* * *

Shaye's hands shook as she clutched her purse and ran through the emergency room to the reception desk, panic biting hard at her heels. "Where's Timmy Grayson?" she asked, her breath catching.

"And you are?"

"I'm Shaye Bartholomew, his legal guardian."

"Oh, I see. Let me check." The woman studied her computer screen. After a few clicks, she announced, "He's in Pediatric ICU."

Shaye had been coming out of the judge's chambers—relieved the judge had determined Jessie would stay in foster care until her mother went through rehab—when her supervisor had appeared, giving her Dylan's message. "He wants you to call the hospital to talk to Dr. Carrera. Something about having your permission to treat Timmy."

Shaye had spoken to the doctor, who had said he wanted to hook Timmy up to an IV and take an X-ray of his lungs. Shaye had agreed, telling him she would be right there.

"Can you page my brother, Randall, and have him meet me in PEDS ICU?"

"I already did that at Mr. Malloy's request."

Without wasting another moment, Shaye spun around and ran into the elevator, stabbing the button a few times. She almost decided to run to the stairs and climb the few flights when the elevator doors swished open. Stepping inside, she tried to control the fear that was making her tremble all over.

She knew her way to PEDS. Timmy had spent time

there after he'd been transferred from the Neonatal Intensive Care Unit.

Walking down the corridor, too many memories came rushing back of the first few days after Timmy had been born...when she'd seen Dylan...when she'd cried in his arms.

She felt so guilty she hadn't stayed home. She felt so guilty she hadn't realized her baby had something more serious than a cold. He wouldn't be here if a cold were the only problem. Dr. Carrera had simply said he was having respiratory distress. That could mean so many things.

Dylan and Randall were outside one of the cubicles, staring in through the glass. Inside, Dr. Carrera stood at the view light, examining X-rays. In the crib, Timmy was hooked up to an IV and oxygen.

"Dylan?" she asked, her voice hardly above a whisper.

When he turned to look at her, his expression was strained. "We don't know what's wrong, yet. He was wheezing, Shaye. Having trouble breathing."

"Oh, my God." She put her hand over her mouth and tried to keep from crying. Dylan didn't comfort her and didn't put his arm around her. He looked as if he were raging his own battle to keep a tight lid on panic. Randall stepped to her side and squeezed her shoulder.

"Did he have a temperature this morning?" Dylan asked. His tone was neutral, not accusatory.

"No. I mean, it was ninety-nine point eight. I thought he just had a little cold." Had he been breathing harder? If she'd put her ear to Timmy's chest, would she have heard wheezing?

Guilt ate at her.

Randall explained, "Barb went home because the kids will be coming home from day camp. You're supposed to call her as soon as you know anything."

Dr. Carrera exited the cubicle as a nurse took a vial from a nearby table and added medication to the IV. Randall pulled Shaye toward a waiting area. Although she wanted to go to Timmy, she knew she had to first hear what Dr. Carrera had to say.

The physician didn't waste any time in explaining. "He has bronchitis, and we're administering antibiotics to ward off secondary infection. We'll see how he does in the next twelve hours."

"It happened so fast," Shaye murmured, not as an excuse but because she still felt dazed being back here in this place where Timmy had fought for his life once before.

The doctor looked at her kindly. "Timmy was a preemie and possibly more susceptible for this to happen. But you can't put a baby in a hermetically sealed bubble. I'll be back to check on him in a few hours. The nurse will page me if there's any change. I'm sorry you have to wait and hope and pray again." He gave her what was meant to be a comforting smile. "I'm sure I'll see you later. You and Dylan can sit with him if you like. No time limit."

After Dr. Carrera left, Randall gave her a hug and kissed her forehead. "I'll give Barb a call. You go in with Timmy. I know that's where you want to be."

Turning to Dylan, she hoped to read the emotion in his eyes but she could only see one—worry. "I'm sorry," she murmured, knowing it had to be said. "I'm so sorry. Maybe you should adopt him. If he had been with you, maybe this wouldn't have happened. At least, if you had had joint custody, they wouldn't have had to wait to treat him."

"There wasn't much of a delay, and this isn't the time to discuss this. Why don't you go in with him? There's a sheaf of papers you have to sign. I'll go get them."

Inside Timmy's cubicle, Shaye pulled a chair close to the crib, sat and kept her hand on Timmy's little arm, needing the contact, praying he could fight off the infection.

At least fifteen minutes later Dylan returned with the papers. He sat by Timmy's bed as she moved to the table across the room and read and signed the documents. The nurse was present more often than not and they didn't talk. After Dylan returned the papers to the desk, he kept a silent vigil with her. Every once in a while their gazes met, but she couldn't stare into those green eyes long, wishing she could read what he was thinking. Whatever bonds had developed between them were clouded now by what had happened to Timmy and their anxiety about him.

While she prayed, Dylan saw to their physical needs and practical concerns. At one point, he brought them coffee and told her he'd contacted Kylie and Gwen. They sent their love. When her brother stopped in for a while, Dylan went to get them something to eat. She told him she wasn't hungry but he insisted she down at least half a sandwich. She did, every bite tasting like cardboard. She was wired enough without the coffee, but she kept drinking it because he brought it.

Before visiting hours ended, Gwen and Kylie stopped by. Dylan encouraged her to take a few minutes to visit with them. As she did, their friendship wrapped around her like the cocoon she needed right now. They assured her they'd stop in again the following day.

Dr. Carrera came in twice, along with a pulmonary physician. Timmy's temperature had dropped to a hundred and two and he took that as a good sign. But Shaye knew her son wasn't out of the woods yet. Throughout the long night, Dylan sat with her, but neither shared their thoughts. All of their attention was focused on Timmy and willing him to get better.

With the change of nurses on the morning shift, Timmy's temperature went down further. It was below one hundred and Dr. Carrera examined him with a smile. "This little guy's a fighter. We've seen that before."

The tightness in Dylan's chest released and gratitude washed through him. He hadn't prayed in years, but last night he'd prayed as he'd never prayed before. He'd been so arrogant to think taking care of a baby was easy. Throughout the night, reality had struck and he'd seen the more conservative side of being a parent, wanting to always keep your child safe and out of harm. He'd practically scoffed at Shaye's fears and now he realized how terribly wrong that had been. In fact, he realized a lot of things. A strong woman, Shaye was almost at her limit after the night of worrying about Timmy.

Dylan saw her chin quiver and then her eyes grow moist, right before she took a deep breath, squared her shoulders and said, "Thank you, Dr. Carrera."

The physician laid a gentle hand on Shaye's shoulder. "Go get something to eat and get some sleep. Both of you. I want to keep Timmy here today, but if all goes well, you can take him home tomorrow."

A nurse was checking Timmy's IV as the doctor left.

Dylan motioned outside. "Let's go sit in the waiting room. There's something I want to ask you."

"All right," Shaye said stoically, as if expecting the worst. Going to Timmy, she kissed him and then stepped outside the cubicle. Dylan walked with her to the waiting area and they sat side by side on the vinyl chairs.

"I know what you're thinking," she said. "That all of this is my fault. I should never have gone to work yesterday. Maybe I can't work and take care of Timmy, too. And we should definitely have joint custody. If I had been delayed in the judge's chambers any longer, what would have happened if the doctor wouldn't treat Timmy without my permission?"

"Stop it, Shaye," Dylan ordered gently. "Kids get sick. Their conditions can change in the blink of an eye. The doctor as much as said that. I don't blame you for what happened. We both need to keep an eye on Timmy, and not just his health, but everything about his life. There's only one way we can do that. We should get married so we can both be full-time parents."

Paling, Shaye stared at him with wide, amazed eyes. "We should get married so we can both be parents?"

"Yes. That's the solution to your work situation and for me spending more time with Timmy. You can stay home with him as long as you want. I can take assignments without worrying if you can handle it all. We can adopt Timmy legally and be real parents."

With a stunned look on her face, she asked, "You say this is a practical solution."

"Yes."

The paleness vanished and color came into Shaye's cheeks then. "If I ever get married, I'll get married because I love a man and he loves me and there's nothing else in this world we want more than to spend our lives together. I won't get married because the arrangement will be convenient, or because I could quit working for a while. I can't marry you just so we can be parents!"

Standing and turning away from him, she said over her shoulder, "I have to make some calls," then hurried down the hall. Her exit was so fast Dylan hardly had time to absorb the fact she was gone because he was still focusing on the fact she'd turned down his proposal.

After a good long cry and a bout of blowing her nose in the ladies' room, Shaye pulled herself together.

Marry Dylan for Timmy's sake.

She simply couldn't. For a moment when Dylan had mentioned marriage, her heart had raced. She'd thought a long-ago forgotten dream might even be in her grasp. But then he'd explained why he was proposing and she'd had to get away from him. Her love for him was one-sided, and a one-sided marriage simply wouldn't work, no matter how practical or convenient.

He wanted to get married because being married would be easier than *not* being married? Because good sex now and then was enough for him?

Now and then.

Their desire was more than now and then.

She shook her head, trying to clear it, trying to reason with herself, reminding herself half a marriage with Dylan would be no marriage at all.

Exiting the ladies' room, she spotted a phone in an alcove and headed for it. Barb and Randall needed to know Timmy had turned a corner.

She was ending her call when she saw her father walking toward her. What was he doing in PEDS? Maybe he had a patient up here.

"Making rounds early?" she asked lightly as he approached her.

"I wanted to see how Timmy was doing."

"How did you know he was sick?"

"I work in this hospital, Shaye. Yesterday, I heard Dr. Carrera paged and then your brother. My sixth sense made me wonder, then I checked the patient roster. I came up here last night before leaving for the day but you and Malloy were with him and I didn't want to intrude."

"You wouldn't have been intruding. I would have appreciated knowing that you cared."

"I care, Shaye. I care that you want to be a mother to this little boy. I was hoping you would have your own children since you were so good with your brothers."

That was the first time her father had ever mentioned the care she'd given her brothers. "Timmy is my own," she replied softly, "even if I have to share him with Dylan."

Her father moved his hand dismissively. "He'll be gone most of the time. You'll be Timmy's parent. How's he doing this morning?"

"Dr. Carrera is moving him to a regular room. He's doing much better. His fever's down."

"Terrific. That baby's been through a lot and so have you." Her father looked uncomfortable, then added, "When he was in the hospital in February, I did visit him."

"I never saw you."

"I know. I wasn't sure how to deal with the whole situation. I didn't want to see you hurt, and if that child didn't make it, you would have been devastated."

The fact that he'd cared about her made her eyes well with tears. Her father simply didn't know how to deal with emotion, but it meant so much to her that he actually *did* care.

Her dad cleared his throat. "Now that you know that Timmy's getting better, would you consider coming over to the house for dinner? Nicole wants to get to know you better."

Studying her dad, she asked, "Are you and Nicole serious?"

"Yes, I think we are. I really can't explain it, Shaye. But she gives me a reason to leave the hospital. In fact, I may consider retiring sooner rather than later. The thing is—she doesn't have any family and she wants to become a part of ours. I know the age difference might be a problem for you—"

"No," she assured him. "The age difference isn't a problem, not if she makes you happy."

Her father smiled. "She does, and she's wise beyond her years. She's making me realize how much I missed with you and Randall and John by working so hard."

A nurse bustled by and when she saw Shaye, she said, "Timmy's in room 305 now."

"Thanks," Shaye called after her.

"Come on," Carson said. "I'll walk you there, then I can take a look at the boy for myself."

As Shaye walked beside her father down the hall, she could sense their relationship was about to change. They might really become father and daughter in the full sense of the words.

Now, if she only knew how to keep her heart from aching when she was around Dylan....

Chapter Fourteen

A half hour later Dylan found himself in the cafeteria, restless and angry. As he sipped another cup of coffee he didn't need, he realized he was angry at himself. He should have waited to bring up marriage until he and Shaye were home with Timmy tucked into bed.

Home. With Shaye.

At that moment, someone pulled out a chair across from him, rattled it and sat down. It was Gwen.

"Do you know what you're doing to Shaye?"

The last thing he needed right now was an argument with one of Shaye's best friends, but it looked as if he and Gwen were headed in that direction.

"What happens between me and Shaye, happens

between me and Shaye. Maybe you shouldn't get involved."

"Not get involved? She's been crying, and *not* over Timmy. She won't talk to me. She always talks to me. When I finally pushed, she told me she doesn't know how to be around you. What did you do to her?"

The impact of Gwen's statement hit him. *She doesn't know how to be around you.*

Did that mean Shaye was going to shut down and close him out? Did that mean even if they had joint custody, Shaye would have her time with Timmy and he would have his?

"I proposed to her," he replied gruffly.

"You what?"

"You heard me." He wasn't in the mood to be diplomatic.

Instead of responding immediately, Gwen stared at the cup of coffee he was turning in his hands, then up at him.

"You don't look a whole lot better than Shaye. Just how did you propose?"

Running a hand over his beard-stubbed chin, he supposed he did look as if he'd been working in the wild. "I asked her to marry me," he returned impatiently. "I told her it would be the best solution for both of us. She wouldn't have to work, and we could both be parents to Timmy."

"No *wonder* she's upset!" Gwen perused him as if he were a criminal. Then she folded her arms in front of her and kept her gaze on his. "Tell me again why you want to marry her."

"I want to marry her because I—" He stopped, forgetting practical reasons. "I don't want to lose anybody else in my life. I want to keep her and Timmy close."

"What does that mean, you want to keep her close?" Gwen prodded.

Reaching deep inside, he let his dreams bubble up to the surface. "I want to wake up with her in the morning and I want to go to bed with her at night. I want to show her places she's never seen before. I want her to be there when I get home, and eventually I want to have kids with her."

"Those reasons have nothing to do with Timmy," Gwen pointed out. After a moment she added, "They aren't terrifically practical reasons, either."

No, they weren't. In fact, practical reasons didn't cause this deep an ache. He had to just *be* with her.

"What do you *feel,* Dylan?"

Shaye's refusal to marry him had torn him in two because he'd begun weaving a life for them. He just hadn't wanted to admit it.

"The people I've cared about—I've lost them."

"Are you afraid if you care too much about Shaye, you'll lose her, too?"

Was he? Had he been using reason and logic and desire to cover up the feeling he didn't want to face? If he loved Shaye, what did that mean to his life? He suddenly stood.

"Dylan?"

"You were just upstairs in Timmy's room?"

"Yes."

"And he's okay?"

"Yes, he's okay."

"I'm going to go back to my place, take a shower and clear my head."

"I tried to convince Shaye that's what she should do but she doesn't want to leave Timmy yet," Gwen admitted.

"When I return, I'll convince her."

"Dylan, I didn't mean to pry."

"Yes, you did. I'm glad Shaye has friends who love her enough to pry. Are you going back up to PEDS?"

"I have a patient to see, but if you want me to give Shaye a message—"

"No message. Anything I have to tell her, I'll tell her myself. Don't worry about her, Gwen. I'm going to make everything right. I just have to figure out the best way to do that."

After she studied him closely for a moment, she nodded, then gave him a small smile. "Good luck."

After Dylan showered at his apartment, he found the answers he needed on his computer monitor as he clicked on one photo after the other. There were pictures of Timmy, but just as many of Shaye. As he studied the photos carefully, he realized he'd tried to capture every one of her expressions, the quirk of her brow as she was surprised by the sight of another horse, her wide smile as she watched foals chasing across the grassland, her wide-eyed awe as the sun descended in a burst of pink and orange behind the mountains, her Madonna-like smile whenever she looked at Timmy. All were faces of Shaye he loved and respected and desired. In the shower, he'd thought about his work and traveling and freedom. Here in the midst of the craft he looked at as a vocation, he saw the future clearly.

Now, if he could just convince Shaye to envision it with him!

After he made a few calls, he took a pair of scissors from the kitchen drawer and went to the yard where he'd seen red roses blooming. Every time he passed them, he thought of Shaye. He cut a perfect bud that was just in the process of opening. After he trimmed off the thorns, he glanced around the backyard. The rose wasn't enough. Adding blooms of larkspur to it, he went to his SUV and drove to the hospital. A few minutes later he was in the elevator, his heart pounding as he waited for the door to open.

As he approached the pediatric wing, he spotted Shaye in the hall talking to a nurse. Peeking into room 305, he saw that Timmy was sleeping. When he headed for Shaye, she heard his footsteps and looked up. He didn't make any attempt to hide the flowers.

The nurse smiled at him. "I was just trying to convince her to go get something to eat."

"I'll take her for breakfast," he assured the woman, clasping Shaye's hand and tugging her toward a vacant room.

"Dylan, what are you doing? I can't just leave."

"I don't want you to leave. I want you to listen to me."

The empty, sterile hospital room wasn't the surroundings he wanted, but it would have to do. "You have to try to do something for me," he told her.

"What?"

"You have to imagine you're on the mountain at night. There's a full moon and millions of stars."

"I don't understand—"

"I know you don't, and that's my fault." He offered her the bouquet. "This is for you. Not for you *and* Timmy, just for you. The flower shops weren't open yet or I would have gotten dozens of flowers, however many it took to prove to you I want to be with you—for *you*. I've lost the people I've loved, Shaye, and for me to admit I was afraid to love again would be a massive understatement. Even though I was trying to protect myself from deeply feeling for someone, I couldn't prevent it. I love you. I want you to marry me so we can share that love, live that love and expand that love. Do you love me?"

He'd never left himself this wide open—so completely vulnerable—before and couldn't quite believe he was doing it now. His future with Shaye was more important than anything in life he'd ever wanted.

Her eyes were shiny and golden as she took the rose with the larkspur and studied the arrangement. Then she lifted her eyes to his. "I do love you, Dylan, but what about your freedom? You need to be free to go where you want to go and do what you want to do."

Shaking his head, he said, "I once thought that was true. I once thought freedom meant no ties. But that kind of freedom comes at too big a price. It carries with it loneliness and restlessness and never having a real home. I want a home with you and Timmy. I looked at my work seriously, and I made a few calls—one to an

old friend who's an editor and the other to my agent.
I'm going to work on two books. First, the wild mustangs in Wyoming, later, the whales off the coast of
Alaska. I'll have to take field trips, but you and Timmy
can come with me.

"Most of my work I'll be doing on my own computer. These projects will take a couple of years, especially if I do some writing with them. I'd like to get
into doing more of that. I've seen Africa. I've photographed Tasmania. I've been to Scotland and Antarctica and Chile. There's plenty of wildlife I can
photograph right here at home. I don't want to be away
from you any more than you want to be away from me,
I hope. And if we have more kids, I can get more
involved in the business of selling prints. I know we
can work it all out, Shaye. Together. Do you want to?
Will you marry me?"

When she threw her arms around his neck, he held
her close. "Is that a yes?"

Leaning back slightly, she looked up at him with all
the love in her heart in her eyes. "Yes, I'll marry you. I
would never expect you to give up the work you love."

Then he kissed her and he knew he had found everything his life had always been missing.

When he broke away, he smiled at her. "When will
you marry me?"

"As soon as there's an opening on the church calendar."

Laughing, he swung her into his arms and spun her
around, knowing he was the luckiest man on earth.

Shaye was laughing, too, holding on to the flowers he'd given her. "I do love you so, Dylan," she breathed.

He kissed her again, intending to prove every day of their lives exactly how worthy a husband and father he could be.

* * * * *

Don't miss Gwen's love story, THE BABY TRAIL,
the next book in
Karen Rose Smith's miniseries BABY BONDS.
Available in July 2006 from
Silhouette Special Edition.

Four sisters.
A family legacy.
And someone is out to destroy it.

A captivating new limited continuity, launching June 2006

The most beautiful hotel in New Orleans,
and someone is out to destroy it. But mystery,
danger and some surprising family revelations
and discoveries won't stop the Marchand sisters
from protecting their birthright...
and finding love along the way.

This riveting new saga begins with

In the Dark

by national bestselling author

JUDITH ARNOLD

The party at Hotel Marchand is in full swing when the lights suddenly go out. What does head of security Mac Jensen do first? He's torn between two jobs—protecting the guests at the hotel and keeping the woman he loves safe.

A woman to protect. A hotel to secure. And no idea who's determined to harm them.

On Sale June 2006

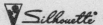

SPECIAL EDITION™

COMING IN JUNE FROM
USA TODAY BESTSELLING AUTHOR

SUSAN MALLERY

HAVING HER BOSS'S BABY

Noelle Stevenson knew she was meant
to be a mom, but she'd hoped to have a
husband first! Then her boss, Devlin Hunter,
proposes a marriage of convenience.
But can they take the heat when their
fake wedding leads to real love?

POSITIVELY PREGNANT:
*Sometimes the unexpected
is the best news of all...*

**Hidden in the secrets of antiquity,
lies the unimagined truth...**

Introducing

ROGUE
Angel™

a brand-new line filled with mystery
and suspense, action and adventure,
and a fascinating look into history.

And it all begins with DESTINY.

In a sealed crypt in
France, where the
terrifying legend of
the beast of Gevaudan
begins to unravel,
Annja Creed discovers
a stunning artifact
that will seal her destiny.

*Available every other
month starting
July 2006, wherever
you buy books.*

GOLD
EAGLE®

GRA1

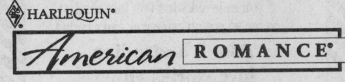

Page-turning drama...

Exotic, glamorous locations...

Intense emotion and passionate seduction...

Sheikhs, princes and billionaire tycoons...

This summer, may we suggest:

THE SHEIKH'S DISOBEDIENT BRIDE
by Jane Porter

On sale June.

AT THE GREEK TYCOON'S BIDDING
by Cathy Williams

On sale July.

THE ITALIAN MILLIONAIRE'S VIRGIN WIFE

On sale August.

With new titles to choose from every month,
discover a world of romance in our books written
by internationally bestselling authors.

HARLEQUIN *Presents*

It's the ultimate in quality romance!

Available wherever Harlequin books are sold.

www.eHarlequin.com

HPGEN06

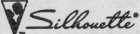

COMING NEXT MONTH

SSECNM0506